The Arabian Nights

Selected Tales

The Classic Adventures Series

First published by Ward Lock & Co. Ltd
This facsimile edition
© Fabbri Publishing Ltd 1992
Printed and bound in Spain by Printer
Industria Gráfica, Barcelona

ISBN 1-85587-337-0

CLASSIC ADVENTURES

This book belongs to

Name . . . .

Date . . . .

CONTENTS

TALES FROM
THE ARABIAN NIGHTS

INTRODUCTION

IN the long, long ago a Sultan, whose name
was Shahriar, ruled over a kingdom as large
as India. He had a wife to whom he was
fondly attached and who, he thought, loved him
fondly in return.

But one day he discovered that his Sultana
cared for him so little that she even preferred
the company of a black slave. His rage on
this discovery was so great that he ordered her
to be put to death, and declared that he would
never again trust a woman.

Consequently, as he did not care to remain
single, he married a new wife every day, and had
her put to death the following morning.

Now the Grand Vizier—that is to say, Prime
Minister—had two daughters, whose names were
Sheherazade and Dinarzade. The elder, in addi-

1   B

tion to being very beautiful, was very accomplished. She had also an amazing memory, and never forgot anything she had read or heard.

In fact, she possessed almost every virtue, and was the apple of her father's eye.

One day, when the Grand Vizier was looking extremely worried because so few suitable young ladies were left, his daughter, Sheherazade, came to him and said :

" My father, I have a favour to ask."

" Ask, my child," he replied, " and if the request is reasonable, which, coming from you, it is sure to be, you may consider it granted."

"Then, my dear father," said Sheherazade, " let *me* be the Sultan's next wife."

The Grand Vizier was at first struck dumb and breathless with horror. When he had recovered, he did his best to induce his daughter to change her mind. But Sheherazade persisted and persuaded and coaxed the poor man until, much against his will, he agreed that she should have her way.

Even the Sultan himself was surprised when the Grand Vizier proposed the match ; for, as he told his Minister plainly, his daughter must not expect to escape the fate which had befallen all the wives who had preceded her.

The Grand Vizier, with tears in his eyes, replied

that both he and his daughter were well aware of this, but that they would, nevertheless, regard the temporary alliance as a great honour.

"In that case," said the Sultan, "the marriage can take place to-morrow."

So, Sheherazade, gorgeously arrayed, was led to the palace. But before she was brought into the presence of the Sultan she called her sister, Dinarzade, aside and said:

"You know what a good story-teller I am? Well, I shall ask the Sultan to let you repose at the foot of the royal couch. Then, just at daybreak, I want you to beg him to allow me to relate one of my stories for the last time."

Dinarzade willingly agreed to this, and the marriage took place.

Now, as before mentioned, Sheherazade was extremely beautiful, and the Sultan was quite charmed with her, and felt almost sorry that he would have to order her to be put to death in the usual way.

Consequently, he willingly consented to allow her to enjoy her sister's company on the last night of her life.

The day was just beginning to break when, according to arrangement, Dinarzade raised her voice and said:

"Oh! my sister, I wonder if His Imperial

Highness would allow you to relate one of your delightful stories ? Never shall I hear anything so good again. Do implore him to let me hear one more tale from your lips before they are closed for ever."

" What is that ? " asked the Sultan sleepily. " Let her tell a story? Why, certainly."

At first he did not pay very much attention to the tale. But, as it went on, he became so enthralled that he felt he simply *must* hear the end ; so, as it was time for him to rise and attend to affairs of state, he decided to put off the execution of Sheherazade for another twenty-four hours, or more if required.

The story of " Ali Baba and the Forty Thieves," and others that follow, were among the tales told by Sheherazade during the " thousand and one nights," for, as we shall see, each successive night brought a story as wonderful as those that had gone before, and the Sultan eventually fell in love with the fair storyteller, and had not the heart to kill her. And everyone will agree that, had he done so, he would have been not only a very wicked but a very foolish man.

SINDBAD THE SAILOR

IN the reign of the Caliph Haroun Alraschid, there lived in Baghdad a poor porter named Hindbad. One day, during the violent heat of summer, when he was carrying a heavy load from one end of the city to the other, he came to a street where the pavement was sprinkled with rose-water, before a large mansion from the windows of which came not only sounds of melody but—which to Hindbad seemed a hundred times better—delicious smells of cooking. A grand feast was in progress, he concluded, and felt some curiosity to know who was the fortunate person to whom the house belonged. He therefore ventured to put the question to some handsomely dressed servants who were standing at the door.

" What," was the reply, " are you an inhabitant of Baghdad, and do not know that this is the residence of Sindbad the sailor, that famous voyager, who has roamed over all the seas under the sun ? "

The porter, who had heard of the immense riches of Sindbad, could not help comparing the situation of this man with his own poverty-stricken condition, and exclaimed in a loud voice : " Almighty Creator of all things, deign to consider the difference there is between Sindbad and myself. I suffer daily a thousand ills, and have the greatest difficulty in supplying my family with bad barley bread, whilst the fortunate Sindbad enjoys every pleasure. What has he done to obtain so happy a destiny, or what crime has been mine to merit a fate so hard ? "

He was still musing on this, when a servant came towards him from the house, and said : " Come, follow me ; my master, Sindbad, wishes to speak with you."

Remembering the words he had uttered, Hindbad feared that Sindbad intended to reprimand him, and therefore tried to excuse himself by declaring that he could not leave his load in the middle of the street. But the servant assured him that it would be taken care of, and pressed him so much that the porter could not very well refuse.

His conductor led him into a spacious room,

where a number of persons were seated round a table, which was covered with all kinds of luxuries. In the principal seat sat a grave and venerable personage, whose long white beard hung down to his breast. This person was Sindbad, to whom the porter made obeisance with fear and trembling. Sindbad desired him to approach, and seating him at his right hand, to his surprise and embarrassment, helped him to the choicest dishes and the finest wine.

Towards the end of the repast, Sindbad inquired the name and profession of his guest.

"Sir," replied the porter, "my name is Hindbad."

"I am happy to see you," said Sindbad, "and I should like you to repeat the words I overheard you utter a little while ago in the street."

At this Hindbad hung his head, and replied: "Sir, I must admit that I uttered some indiscreet words, which I entreat you to pardon."

"Oh," resumed Sindbad, "do not imagine I am so unjust as to have any resentment on that account; but I must undeceive you on one point. You appear to suppose that the riches and comforts I enjoy have been obtained without labour or trouble. You are mistaken. Before attaining my present position, I have endured the greatest mental and bodily sufferings you can possibly imagine. Perhaps you have heard only a confused account of my adventures in the seven voyages I have made, and as an opportunity now offers, I will relate to you and the rest of this honourable company some of the dangers I have encountered. Listen then to the history of my first voyage."

THE FIRST VOYAGE.

I squandered the greater part of the fortune I inherited from my father in youthful dissipation ; but at length I saw my folly, and resolved to collect the small remains of my inheritance and employ it profitably in trade. This I did, and then repaired to Basra, where I embarked with several merchants in a vessel which had been equipped at our joint expense.

We set sail, and steered towards the Indies, by the Persian Gulf, touching at several islands, where we sold or exchanged our merchandise. One day, we were unexpectedly becalmed before a little green island which was of a most attractive appearance. The captain gave permission to those passengers who wished it to go ashore, and of this number I formed one. But, while we were enjoying ourselves, the island suddenly trembled, and we felt a severe shock.

Those who had remained in the ship immediately called to us to re-embark, or we should perish ; for what we supposed to be an island was really the back of a great whale. The most active of the party jumped into the boat, whilst others threw themselves into the water, to swim to the ship. As for me, I was still on the island, or, more properly speaking, on the whale, when it dived below the surface, and I had only time to seize a piece of wood which had been brought to make a fire with, when the monster disappeared beneath the waves. Meanwhile, the captain, anxious to avail himself of a fair breeze which had sprung up, set sail with those who had reached his vessel, and left me to the mercy of the waves. I remained in this deplorable situation the whole of that day and the following night. On the return of morning I had neither strength nor hope left ; but when I was at my last gasp a breaker happily threw me on to an island.

Much weakened by fatigue, I crept about in search of some herb or fruit that might satisfy my hunger. I found some, and had also the good luck to discover a stream of excellent water. Feeling much stronger, I began to explore the island, and entered a beautiful plain, where I perceived some fine horses grazing. Whilst I was admiring them, a man appeared who asked me who I was. I related my adventure to him ; whereupon he led me into a cave, where I found some other persons, who were not less astonished to see me than I was to meet them.

I ate some food which they offered me ; and upon my asking them what they did there, they replied that they were grooms to the King of that island, and the horses were brought there once a year for the sake of the excellent pasturage. They told me that the morrow was the day fixed for their departure, and if I had been one day later I must certainly have perished ; because they lived so far off that it would have been impossible for me to have found my way without a guide.

The following day they returned, with the horses, to the capital of the island, whither I accompanied them. On our arrival the King, to whom I related my story, gave orders that I should be taken care of and supplied with everything I might want.

As I was a merchant, I associated with persons of my own profession, in the hope of meeting someone with whom I could return to Baghdad ; for the capital of the King is situated on the sea-coast, and has a beautiful port, where vessels from all parts of the world daily arrive.

As I was standing one day near the port, I saw a ship come towards the land. When the crew had cast anchor, they began to unload its goods. Happening to cast my eyes on some of the packages, I saw my name written thereon, and recognized them as those which I had embarked in the ship in which I left Basra. I also recognized the captain, and asked him to whom those parcels belonged.

" I had on board with me," replied he, " a merchant of Baghdad, named Sindbad. One day, when we were near an island, or at least what appeared to be one, he went ashore with some other passengers. But this supposed island was nothing but an enormous whale that had fallen asleep on the surface of the water. The monster no sooner felt the heat of a fire they lighted on its back to cook their provisions, than it began to move and flounce about in the sea. Most of the persons who were on it were drowned, and the unfortunate Sindbad was one of the number. These parcels belonged to him ; and I have resolved to sell them, that if I meet with any of his family I may be able to pay over to them the profit I shall have made."

" Captain," said I then, " I am that Sindbad whom you supposed dead, but who is still alive ; and these parcels are my property."

When the captain heard me speak thus he exclaimed : " That is impossible. With my own eyes I saw Sindbad perish ; the passengers I had on board were also witnesses of his death. And now you have the assurance to say that *you* are that same Sindbad ? At first sight you appeared a man of probity and honour ; yet you are not above telling an outrageous falsehood in order to possess yourself of merchandise which does not belong to you."

" Have patience," replied I, " and listen to what I have to say."

I then related in what manner I had been saved, and by what lucky accident I found myself in this part of the country.

The captain was rather staggered at first, but was soon convinced that I was not an impostor. Then, embracing me, he exclaimed : " Heaven be praised that you have escaped. Here are your goods ; take them, for they are yours." I thanked him, and selected the most precious and valuable things in my bales as presents for the King, to whom I related the manner in which I had recovered my property. He accepted the presents, and gave me others of far greater value. Hereupon I took my leave, and re-embarked in the same vessel in which I had first set out ; having first exchanged what merchandise remained for aloes, sandal wood, camphor, nutmegs, cloves, pepper, ginger, and other products of the country. We touched at several islands, and at last landed at Basra, from whence I came here. And, as I had realized about a hundred thousand gold pieces as the result of my voyage, I determined to forget the hardships I had endured, and to enjoy the pleasures of life."

Having thus concluded the story of his first voyage, Sindbad ordered a purse containing a hundred gold pieces to be brought him, and gave it to the porter, saying: "Take this, Hindbad; return to your home, and come again to-morrow, to hear the continuation of my history."

The porter returned home, and the account he gave of his adventure to his wife and family made them call down many blessings on the head of Sindbad.

On the following day, Hindbad dressed himself in his best clothes, and betook himself to the house of Sindbad, who received him in a friendly manner. As soon as the guests had all arrived the feast was served, and when it was over, Sindbad said: "My friends, I will now give you an account of my second voyage."

THE SECOND VOYAGE.

As I told you yesterday, I had resolved to pass the rest of my days in peace at Baghdad. But the desire to travel returned ; so I bought some goods, and set sail with other merchants, to seek fortune.

We went from island to island, bartering our goods very profitably. One day, we landed on one which was covered with a variety of fruit trees, but we could not discover any habitation, or the trace of a human being. Whilst some of my companions were amusing themselves by gathering fruits and flowers, I seated myself under some trees and fell asleep. I cannot say how long I slept, but when I rose to look for my companions, they were all gone ; and I could only just descry the vessel in full sail, at such a distance that I soon lost sight of it.

After some moments given to despair, I climbed a high tree to look about me; and, gazing around on land and sea, my eye was caught by a large white spot in the distance. I climbed down quickly, and, making my way towards the object, found it to be a ball of prodigious size. When I got near enough to touch it, I found it was soft and so smooth that any attempt to climb it would have been fruitless. Its circumference might be about fifty paces.

The sun was then near setting, and suddenly it seemed to be obscured, as by a cloud. I was surprised at this change; but how much did my amazement increase, when I perceived it to be occasioned by a bird of most extraordinary size, which was flying towards me. I recollected having heard sailors speak of a bird called a roc; and I concluded that the great white ball which had drawn my attention must be the egg of this bird. I was not mistaken; for shortly afterwards the bird lighted on the white ball, and seated itself upon it. When I saw this huge fowl coming, I drew near to the egg, so that I had one of the claws of the bird just before me; this claw was as big as the trunk of a large tree. I tied myself to the claw with the linen of my turban, in hopes that the roc, when it took its flight the next morning, would carry me with it out of that desert island. My project succeeded; for at break of day the roc flew away, and bore me to such a height that I could no longer distinguish the earth; then it descended with such rapidity that I almost lost my senses. When the roc had alighted, I quickly untied the knot that bound me to its foot, and had scarcely released myself when it darted on a serpent of immeasurable length, and, seizing the snake in its beak, flew away.

The place in which the roc left me was a very deep valley, surrounded on all sides by mountains of such height that their summits were lost in the clouds, and so steep that there was no possibility of climbing them.

As I walked along this valley, I remarked that it was strewn with diamonds, some of which were of astonishing size. I amused myself for some time by examining them; but soon perceived from afar some objects which destroyed my pleasure, and created in me great fear. These were a great number of enormous serpents, to escape from which I retired into a cave, the entrance of which I closed with a stone, and where I ate what remained of the provisions I had brought from the ship. All night long I could hear the terrible hissing of the serpents, which retired to their lairs at sunrise, when I left my cave with trembling, and may truly say that I walked a long time on diamonds without feeling the least desire to possess them. At last, I sat down and fell asleep, for I had not once closed my eyes during the previous night. I had scarcely begun to doze, when the noise of something falling awoke me. It was a large piece of fresh meat; and at the same moment I saw a number of other pieces rolling down the rocks from above.

I had always disbelieved the accounts I had heard from seamen and others of the Valley of Diamonds, and of the means by which merchants procured these precious gems. I now knew it to be true. The method is this : the merchants go to the mountains which surround the valley, cut large pieces of meat, and throw them down ; and the diamonds on which the lumps of meat fall stick to them. The eagles, which are larger and stronger in that country than in any other, seize these pieces of meat, to carry to their young at the top of the rocks. The merchants then run to the eagles' nests, oblige the birds to retreat, and then take the diamonds that have stuck to the pieces of meat.

I had begun to look on this valley as my tomb ; but now felt a little hope. I therefore collected the largest diamonds I could find, and with these filled the leather bag in which I had carried my provisions. I then took one of the largest pieces of meat, tied it tightly round me with my turban, and laid myself on the ground.

I had not been long in this position before the eagles began to descend, and each seized a piece of meat, with which it flew away. One of the strongest darted on the piece to which I was attached, and carried me up with it to its nest. The merchants then began their cries to frighten

away the eagles ; and when they had obliged
the birds to quit their prey, one of them approached, but was much surprised and alarmed
on seeing me. He soon, however, recovered from
his fear, and began to quarrel with me for
trespassing on what he called his property.

" You will speak to me with pity instead of
anger," said I, " when you learn by what means
I reached this place. Console yourself ; for I
have diamonds for you as well as for myself ;
and my diamonds are more valuable than those
of all the other merchants together."

Saying this, I showed him my store. I had
scarcely finished speaking, when the other merchants, perceiving me, flocked round with great
astonishment ; and their wonder was still greater
when I related my history, and showed my
diamonds, which they declared to be unequalled
in size and quality.

As all were now contented with their share
of the diamonds which I distributed among them,
we set out next day, travelling over high mountains, which were infested by large serpents ;
but we had the good fortune to escape them.
We reached the nearest port, where I exchanged
some of my diamonds for valuable merchandise ;
and at last, after having touched at several ports,
we reached Basra, from which place I returned
to Baghdad.

Here Sindbad closed the relation of his second voyage. He again ordered a hundred pieces of gold to be given to Hindbad, whom he invited to come on the morrow ; when, the usual repast ended, he began to tell the story of his third voyage.

THE THIRD VOYAGE.

I soon forgot the dangers I had encountered in my two voyages, and, tired of doing nothing, again set sail with merchandise from Basra.

After a long voyage, during which we touched at several ports, we were overtaken by a violent tempest, which made us lose our reckoning. The storm continued for several days, and drove us near an island where we were compelled to cast anchor, in spite of the fact that it was inhabited by a very savage race of dwarfs. Their number was so great that the captain warned us to make no resistance, or they would pour upon us like locusts, and destroy us. This information, which alarmed us very much, proved only too true; for very soon we saw advancing a multitude of hideous savages, entirely covered with red hair, and about two feet high. They threw themselves into the sea, swam to the ship, and soon came swarming on the deck.

Unfurling the sails, they cut the cable, and

after dragging the ship ashore, obliged us to disembark.

We left the shore, and, penetrating into the island, found some fruits and herbs, which we ate in fear and trembling. As we walked, we perceived at a distance a great building, towards which we bent our steps. It was a large and lofty palace, with folding gates of ebony, which opened as we pushed them. We entered the courtyard, and saw, facing us, a vast apartment, with a vestibule, on one side of which was a large heap of human bones, while on the opposite side appeared a number of spits for roasting.

The sun was setting; and while we were still paralysed with horror, the door of the apartment suddenly opened with a loud noise, and there entered a black man of frightful aspect, as tall as a large palm-tree. In the middle of his forehead gleamed a single eye, red and fiery as a burning coal; his front teeth were long and sharp, and projected from his mouth, which was as wide as that of a horse; his ears resembled those of an elephant, and covered his shoulders, and his long and curved nails were like the talons of an immense bird. At this sight we almost lost our senses; and when, after closely examining us, he seized me and began to pinch me all over, I felt that I was as good as dead.

Fortunately, he found me too skinny, so, dropping me, he seized the captain, who was the fattest of the party, and, spitting him like a sparrow, he roasted and ate him for his supper. He then went to sleep, snoring louder than thunder.

He did not wake till the next morning; but we passed the night in the most agonizing suspense. When daylight returned, the giant awoke, and went abroad, leaving us in the palace.

We sought to escape, but could find no way. Towards evening the giant returned and supped upon another of my unfortunate companions; he then slept, snored, and departed, as before, at daybreak.

Our situation was so hopeless that some were on the point of throwing themselves into the sea. But I dissuaded them, as I had a project which I proceeded to impart to them.

" My friends," said I, " you know that there is a great deal of wood on the seashore. Let us get some rafts in readiness, and then take the first opportunity of executing the plan I have thought of." My advice was approved by all; and we immediately built some rafts, each large enough to support three persons. These rafts we carefully concealed.

On the giant's return, another of our party

was sacrificed. But we were soon revenged on him for his cruelty. As soon as we heard him snore, I and nine of the most courageous amongst us, took each a spit, and making the points red hot, thrust them into his eye, and blinded him.

The pain made him groan hideously. He threw his arms about on all sides, to try and catch us, but we were able to avoid him. At last he found the door, and went out, bellowing with pain.

We at once ran to the shore where our rafts lay; but were obliged to wait until daybreak before embarking.

The sun had scarcely risen, however, when, to our horror, we saw our cruel enemy, led by two giants nearly as huge as himself, and accompanied by several others, coming towards us.

We immediately ran to our rafts and rowed away as fast as possible. The giants, seeing this, picked up some huge stones, and, wading into the sea to their waists, hurled them at the rafts, and sank all but the one I was on. Thus I and two companions were the only men who escaped.

As we rowed with all our strength, we were soon beyond reach of the stones, and gained the open sea, where we were tossed about for a day and a night. We then had the good fortune to be thrown on an island, where we found some excellent fruit, which soon recruited our exhausted strength.

When night came on, we went to sleep on the seashore, but were soon awakened by the noise made by the hissing of an immense serpent, which devoured one of my companions before he had time to escape.

My other comrade and myself took to flight, and during the day, noticing a very high tree, climbed it, hoping to spend the night there in safety. The hissing of the serpent again warned us of its approach, and, twining itself round the trunk, it swallowed my unfortunate companion, who was on a lower branch than myself, and then retired.

I remained on the tree till daybreak, when I descended, more dead than alive.

However, towards evening, I collected a great quantity of wood and furze, and, tying it in faggots, placed it in a circle round the tree; then, tying another bundle upon my head, I sat down within the circle. The serpent returned with the intention of devouring me, but, though he watched and waited the whole night, was prevented from approaching me by the rampart I had formed. He retired at sunrise; but I felt that death would be preferable to such another night of horror, and so ran towards the sea. But, as I was about to cast myself in, I saw a ship at a distance. I cried out with all my strength, and unfolded and waved my turban, to attract the attention of those on board. It did so, and the captain sent a boat to bring me off.

All on board were amazed at the story of my marvellous escape, and treated me with the greatest kindness and generosity.

One day, the captain called me and said: " Brother, I have in my possession some goods which belonged to a merchant who was a passenger on my ship. As he is dead, I am going to have them valued, that I may render an account of them to the heirs of this man, whose name was Sindbad. In this task I shall be glad of your assistance."

At this, I looked at the captain in amazement, and recognized him as the one who on my second voyage had left me asleep on the island.

We were both of us changed in appearance; which accounted for neither at first recognizing the other. But, on my declaring myself, he remembered me, and begged my forgiveness for the error by which I had been abandoned. " God be praised for your escape," cried he. " Here are your goods, which I have preserved with care, and now have the greatest pleasure in restoring to you."

And so, at length, with all this additional wealth, I landed at Basra, and came from there to Baghdad.

Sindbad thus finished the history of his third voyage. Again he gave Hindbad a hundred gold pieces, inviting him to the usual repast on the morrow, when he continued the story of his adventures.

THE FOURTH VOYAGE.

In spite of the terrible dangers I had encountered on my third voyage, it was not long before I tired of the land, and again set sail with merchandise, as before.

All went well until one day we met with a sudden squall, and were driven on a sandbank, where the boat went to pieces, and a number of the crew perished.

I and some others had the good fortune to get hold of a plank, on which we drifted to an island where we found fruit and fresh water, with which we refreshed ourselves and then lay down to sleep.

The next morning, when the sun was risen, we left the shore, and walking inland, saw some dwellings towards which we made our way.

But they proved to be inhabited by a number of blacks, who took us prisoners, and made all but myself eat of a certain herb.

I refused, as I had a presentiment of some evil purpose ; and I was right, for my companions shortly became light-headed, and did not know what they said or did.

Then a meal of rice cooked in cocoanut oil was offered us, of which I ate very sparingly, but which the others devoured ravenously. This rice was to fatten us ; for we had the terrible misfortune to have fallen into the hands of cannibals, who intended to feast on us when we were in good condition.

And so, one by one, my poor companions, who had lost their senses and could not foresee their fate, were devoured ; while I, who ate next to nothing, became daily thinner and less palatable.

In the meantime, I was allowed a great deal of liberty; and one day took the opportunity to escape. I walked for seven days, taking care to avoid those places which appeared to be inhabited, and living on cocoanuts, which afforded me both drink and food.

On the eighth day I came to the seashore, where I saw some white people employed in gathering pepper, which grew very plentifully in that place, and who, as soon as I approached them, asked me in Arabic whence I came.

Delighted to hear my native language once more, I readily satisfied their curiosity; and when they embarked I went with them to the island from which they had come. I was presented to their King, who was astonished at the story of my adventures, and took me into favour, and treated me with such kindness that I almost forgot my previous misfortunes.

I remarked one thing which appeared to me very singular; every one, the King not excepted, rode on horseback without saddle, bridle, or stirrups. I one day took the liberty to ask his Majesty why such things were not used in his city; he replied that he had never heard of the articles of which I spoke.

I immediately went to a workman, and gave him a model from which to make the tree of a saddle. When he had executed his task, I myself covered the saddle-tree with leather, richly embroidered in gold, and stuffed it with hair. I then applied to a locksmith, who made me a bit and some stirrups according to the patterns I gave him.

These things I presented to the King, who was highly delighted with them, and, as a sign of his favour, bestowed upon me, as a wife, a lady, beautiful, rich and accomplished, with whom I lived happily for some time, though I often thought regretfully of my native city of Baghdad, and longed to return there.

One day, the wife of one of my neighbours, with whom I was very intimate, fell sick and died. I went to console the widower, and, finding him in the deepest affliction, said to him : " May God preserve you, and grant you a long life."

" Alas ! " replied he, " I have only one hour to live. This very day, according to the custom of the country, I shall be buried with my wife."

While I was still mute with horror at this barbarous custom, his relations and friends came to make arrangements for the funeral. They dressed the corpse of the woman as though for her bridal, and decorated her with jewels ; then they placed her on an open bier, and the procession set out. The husband, dressed in mourning, went next, and the relations followed. They took their way to a high mountain, on the summit of which was a deep pit covered with a large stone, into which the body was lowered. The husband, to whom was given a jug of water and seven small loaves, then took leave of his friends and allowed himself to be lowered into the pit, and the stone was replaced.

I was much affected by this, and expressed my horror to the King. " What can I do, Sindbad ? " he replied. " It is a law common to all ranks, and even I submit to it. I shall be interred alive with the queen, my consort, if she happens to die first."

" And must strangers submit to this cruel custom ? " I asked.

" Certainly," said the King, " they are not exempt when they marry in the island."

After this, you may imagine my distress when my wife died after a few days' illness. I almost regretted that I had not been eaten by the cannibals; and though the funeral procession was honoured by the presence of the King and his whole court, I was not in the least consoled, and followed the body of my wife, deploring my miserable destiny. At the last moment I tried to save my life by pleading my position as a stranger ; but in vain. I was lowered into the pit, with my seven loaves and jug of water, and the stone was replaced on the opening.

In spite of the horrors of my situation, I lived for some days on my provisions. But one day, when they were exhausted, and I was preparing to die of starvation, I heard a sound of loud breathing, together with footsteps. I felt my way in that direction, and saw a shadow which fled before me. I pursued it until, at last, I perceived a small speck of light resembling a star, and kept on towards it till I arrived at an opening in the rock, through which I scrambled and found myself on the seashore. Then I discovered that the object I had followed was a small animal, which lived among the rocks.

I cannot describe my joy at this escape. But, after a time, I ventured to return to the cave and collect a great quantity of jewels and gold ornaments, which had been buried with the dead. These I secured about me, and then returned to the shore in time to see a ship approaching.

I managed to attract attention by shouting and waving my turban, was taken on board, and at length arrived once more in safety at Baghdad.

Sindbad here concluded the relation of his fourth voyage. He repeated his present of a hundred gold coins to Hindbad, whom he requested, with the rest of the company, to return on the following day, when he began the account of his fifth voyage.

THE FIFTH VOYAGE.

It was not long before the peaceful and pleasant life I led palled upon me. This time, I built a vessel of my own, on which I took several other merchants as passengers; and we set sail with a fair wind and a rich cargo. The first place we stopped at was a desert island, where we found the egg of a roc, as large as that of which I spoke on a former occasion. It contained a small roc, almost hatched; for its beak had begun to pierce the shell. My companions, in spite of my advice, broke open the egg with hatchets, and roasted the young bird, bit by bit.

They had scarcely finished their meal, when two immense clouds appeared in the air at a considerable distance. The captain cried out that the father and mother of the young roc were coming, and warned us to re-embark as quickly as possible, to escape the danger which threatened us. We took his advice, and set sail immediately.

The two rocs approached, uttering the most terrible screams, which they redoubled on finding their egg broken and their young one destroyed. They then flew away towards the mountains whence they had come, and we hoped we had seen the last of them.

But they soon returned, each with an enormous piece of rock in its claws, which, when they were directly over our ship, they let fall. Our ship was smashed, and all on board, with the exception of myself, either crushed to death or drowned.

I was under water for some time, but, coming to the surface, was able to seize a piece of wreckage, by the aid of which I reached an island on which I landed with some difficulty.

When I had rested awhile, I proceeded farther inland, and was charmed by the beauty of all I saw. I ate of the ripe fruits which hung from the trees on every side, and drank of the crystal streams.

When night came I lay down to rest on a mossy bank; and when the sun rose I continued my way until I came to a little rivulet, beside which I saw an aged man seated.

I saluted him, and asked what he was doing there; but, instead of answering, he made signs to me to take him on my shoulders, and cross the brook, making me understand that he wanted to gather some fruit upon the other side.

Accordingly, taking him on my back, I waded through the stream. When I had reached the other side, I stooped for him to alight; instead of which he clambered on to my shoulders, crossed his legs round my neck, and gripped me so tightly round the throat that I was nearly strangled, and fell to the ground.

But he still kept his place on my shoulders, and kicked me so hard that I was forced to rise. He then made me walk under some trees, the fruit of which he gathered and ate. He never quitted his hold during the day ; and at night he laid himself on the ground, still clinging to my neck.

From this time forward I was his beast of burden, all attempts to dislodge him being vain, until, one day, I chanced to find on the ground several dried gourds, which had fallen from the tree that bore them. I took a large one, and, after having cleared it out, I squeezed into it the juice of several bunches of grapes, which the island produced in great abundance. This I left in a particular spot for some days, when, returning, I found the juice converted into wine.

I drank some of it, and it had such an exhilarating effect that, in spite of my burden, I began to dance and sing. Noticing this, the old man indicated that he also wished to taste the liquor, which he liked so well that he emptied the gourd. The wine went almost immediately to his head, and he began to sway to and fro on my shoulders. Before long his grasp relaxed, and I was able to throw him to the ground, where I despatched him with a blow from a big stone.

I was much rejoiced at having got rid of this old man, and set out towards the seashore, where I met some people who belonged to a vessel which had anchored there to get fresh water. They were much astonished at seeing me and hearing the account of my adventure.

" You had fallen," said they, " into the hands of the Old Man of the Sea, and you are the first of his captives whom he has not strangled sooner or later. On that account the sailors and merchants who land here never dare approach except in a strong body."

They then took me to their ship, and, sailing with them, in a few days we anchored in the harbour of a large city.

One of the merchants on the ship had become on very friendly terms with me. On landing he gave me a large sack, and then introduced me to some others who were also furnished with sacks, and said : " Go, follow these people, and do as they do."

We set off together, and arrived at a large forest of cocoanut trees, the trunks of which were so smooth that it was impossible for any to climb them but the monkeys who lived among the branches.

My companions then collected stones, which they threw at the monkeys, who retaliated by hurling cocoanuts; and, in this way, we easily obtained enough to fill our sacks.

By selling these nuts to merchants in the city, in the course of time I made a considerable sum.

I then obtained a passage in a ship which

called for a cargo of cocoanuts, and which was bound for the Island of Kamari, which was celebrated for its pearl fishery.

Here I hired divers, and was so fortunate as to obtain a number of fine pearls, with which I again set sail, and landed at Basra, having still further increased my riches, a tenth part of which I bestowed in charity, as was now my custom on returning from a voyage.

At the end of this narrative Sindbad, as usual, gave a hundred pieces of gold to Hindbad, who retired with all the other guests. The same party returned the next day; and after their host had regaled them in as sumptuous a manner as on the preceding days, he began the account of his sixth voyage.

THE SIXTH VOYAGE.

ABOUT a year after my return from my fifth voyage, I again embarked on a ship, the captain of which intended to make a long voyage.

Long indeed it proved; for the captain and pilot lost their way, and did not know how to steer. When, at last, the captain discovered our whereabouts, he threw his turban on the deck, tore his beard and beat his head, like a man distraught.

On being asked the reason for this behaviour,

he replied, " We are in the greatest peril. A rapid current is hurrying the ship along, and we shall all perish in less than a quarter of an hour. Pray Allah to deliver us from this dreadful danger; for nothing can save us unless He takes pity on us."

He then gave orders to hoist more sail; but the ropes broke in the attempt, and the ship becoming quite unmanageable, was dashed by the current against a rock, where it split and went to pieces. Nevertheless, we had time to disembark our provisions, as well as the most valuable part of the cargo.

When we were assembled on the shore the captain said: " Allah's will be done. Here we may dig our graves; for we are in a place so desolate that no one cast on this shore has ever returned to his own home."

The mountain, at the foot of which we were, formed part of an island, the coast of which was covered with wreckage and all kinds of valuable merchandise in bales and chests which had been thrown up by the sea. Indeed, if we could have lived on gold or jewels, all might have been well. As it was, starvation was bound to overcome us before very long.

One strange thing in connection with the place was a river of fresh water which ran from the sea and disappeared into a cavern of the mountain.

We remained on the shore in a hopeless condition; for the mountain was too steep to climb, and we were thus without any means of escape. And so the fate we feared gradually overcame us. Those who died first were interred by the others, and I had the dismal office of burying my last companion; for I had eaten more sparingly of my share of the stock of provisions which had been divided among us, and so held out the longest. Nevertheless, when I buried the last of them, I had so little food left that I imagined I must soon follow him.

But Allah had pity on me, and inspired me with the thought of examining the river which lost itself in the recesses of the cave. Having done so, I decided to make a raft, and trust myself to the current, and see where it would take me. If I perished, it was but altering the manner of my death.

I set to work at once, and made a strong framework of wood bound with rope, of which there was abundance scattered about the shore. I then selected the chests containing the most valuable jewels and stuffs among the wreckage; and when I had carefully stowed all these things so as to balance the raft, I embarked on my vessel, guiding it with the little oar which I had provided, and resigned myself to Providence.

The current carried me under the vault of the cavern; and I soon found myself in darkness, and rowed, for what appeared to be days, without perceiving a single ray of light.

During this time, I consumed the last of my hoarded stock of provisions. I then either fell asleep, or became unconscious; but when I came to I was surprised to find myself in an open country, near a bank of the river, to which my raft was fastened, and surrounded by a number of negroes.

I felt so overcome with joy that I could scarcely believe myself awake. Being, at length, convinced that my deliverance was not a dream, I gave thanks aloud; on which one of the negroes, who understood Arabic, advanced and said:

" Do not be alarmed at the sight of us. The river which issues from yonder mountain is that from which we get water for our fields. When we saw your raft being borne towards us, we swam to it, and guided it to shore. And now I beg you to tell us whence you came."

I replied: " I will do so, with pleasure, when I have eaten; for I am at the point of starvation."

I satisfied my hunger, and then proceeded to satisfy their curiosity; after which they declared they must take me to their King. So, having procured a horse for me, they hauled my raft ashore, and followed me with it on their shoulders to the city of Serendib, where their King received me with great kindness.

To him I related all that had befallen me; and he was so pleased with the history of my adventures that he ordered it to be written in letters of gold, and preserved among the archives of his kingdom. The raft was then produced, and, prostrating myself before him, I said: " If your Majesty will honour me by accepting my cargo, the whole is at your disposal."

But, although he smiled, and appeared pleased, he refused my offer, and said that when I left his kingdom I should carry with me proof of his regard.

After I had spent some days examining the city and its surroundings, I begged to be allowed to return to my own country. The King not only gave me permission, together with a gift of great value, but also did me the high honour of entrusting me with a letter and gifts for the Caliph Haroun Alraschid.

These gifts included a vase made of a single ruby, filled with pearls, and a female slave of marvellous beauty, who wore jewels worth a king's ransom.

After a long but fortunate voyage, we landed

at Basra, whence I returned to Baghdad, and at once executed my commission, and presented the letter and the gifts of the King of Serendib to the Caliph, who, after he had put a number of questions to me concerning the country from which I had returned, dismissed me with a handsome present.

Sindbad here finished his discourse, and his visitors retired, Hindbad, as usual, receiving his hundred gold pieces. The guests and the porter returned on the following day, and Sindbad began the relation of his seventh and last voyage.

THE SEVENTH AND LAST VOYAGE.

I now determined, as I was past the prime of life, to go to sea no more, but enjoy a pleasant and reposeful existence at home.

But one day the Caliph sent for me.

" Sindbad," he said, " I want you to do me a service. You must go once more to the King of Serendib with my answer and presents ; for it is but right that I should make him a proper return for the civility he has shown me."

" Commander of the Faithful," I replied, " I humbly entreat you to consider that I am worn out with the fatigues I have undergone in my six voyages. I have even made a vow never again to leave Baghdad."

I then took occasion to relate the long history of my adventures. When I had done speaking, the Caliph said : " I confess that these are extraordinary adventures ; nevertheless, they must not prevent you from making the voyage I propose, which is only to the island of Serendib. You must be sensible that it would be beneath my dignity if I remained under obligation to the King of that island."

As I plainly saw that the Caliph had resolved on my going, I signified that I was ready to obey his commands ; whereat he provided me with a thousand pieces of gold to pay the expenses of the voyage.

In a few days, having received the presents from the Caliph, together with a letter written with his own hand, I set off to Basra, where I embarked and, after a pleasant voyage, arrived at the island of Serendib.

I soon obtained an audience with the King, who showed pleasure at the sight of me. " Welcome, Sindbad," said he ; " I assure you I have often thought of you since your departure. Blessed be this day in which I see you again."

After thanking the King for his kindness, I delivered the letter and present of the Caliph, which he received with every mark of pleasure. The Caliph had sent him a complete bed of gold tissue, fifty robes of a very rare stuff, a hundred more of the finest white linen, a bed of crimson velvet, and another of a different pattern and colour. Besides this, he sent a vase of agate, carved in the most wonderful manner.

Soon after this, I requested leave to depart, which the King granted; at the same time giving me a handsome present. I then re-embarked; but three or four days after we had set sail we were attacked by pirates, who easily made themselves masters of our vessel. Those who attempted resistance lost their lives. I and all those who had the prudence to submit quietly were made slaves. After they had stripped us, and clothed us in rags instead of our own garments, the pirates bent their course towards a distant island, where they sold us.

I was purchased by a rich merchant, who took me home with him. Some days later, he asked me if I could shoot with a bow and arrow.

I replied that I had practised that sport in my youth, and that I did not think I had entirely lost my skill. He then gave me a bow and some arrows, and, making me mount behind him on an elephant, took me to a vast forest some hours' journey from the city. We went a great way into the forest, till the merchant came to a particular spot, where he made me alight. Then he showed me a large tree. " Climb that tree," said he, " and shoot at the elephants that pass under it ; for there are many of these animals in this forest. If one should fall, come and let me know."

Thereupon, he left me some provisions, and returned to the city.

During the first night no elephants came ; but the next day, as soon as the sun had risen, a great number made their appearance. I shot many arrows at them, and at last one fell. The others immediately retired, and left me at liberty to go and inform my master of my success.

He praised me and, returning with me, we dug a pit and buried the elephant, so that the body might rot and the tusks be more easily secured.

I continued my new occupation for two months ; and not a day passed in which I did not kill an elephant. But one day, instead of passing on as usual, the elephants herded together and came towards me, trumpeting loudly, and in such numbers that the ground trembled under their tread. They approached my tree, and surrounded it with their trunks extended, and their eyes all fixed upon me. At this surprising spectacle I was so unnerved that my bow and arrows fell from my hands.

After the elephants had viewed me for some time, one of the largest twisted his trunk round the body of the tree, tore it up by the roots and threw it on the ground. I fell with the tree; but the animal took me up with his trunk, and placed me on his shoulders, where I lay more dead than alive. The huge beast now put himself at the head of his companions, and carried me to a little hill, where he set me down, and then went away with the rest.

After I had waited some time, seeing no other elephants, I arose, and perceived that the hill was entirely covered with bones and tusks of elephants. Evidently, this was their cemetery, and they had brought me hither to show it me, that I might desist from destroying them merely for the sake of possessing their tusks. I did not stay there long, but turned my steps towards the city, and, after walking for a day and a night, arrived at my master's.

As soon as he saw me, he exclaimed:

" Ah, my poor Sindbad! I have been wondering what could have become of you. I have been to the forest, where I found a tree newly torn up by the roots, and your bow and arrows on the ground. And so I despaired of ever seeing you again. Pray tell me by what fortunate chance you are still alive."

I satisfied his curiosity; and the following day he accompanied me to the hill, and, with great joy, convinced himself of the truth of my story. We loaded the elephant on which we had come with as many tusks as it could carry; and when we returned my master said:

"Brother, I give you your liberty. We have not hitherto been able to get ivory without risking the lives of our slaves; now our whole city will be enriched by your means; and I shall take care that you are rewarded accordingly."

To this I replied: "The only recompense I desire is permission to return to my own country."

"Well," he replied, "you will have an opportunity shortly, for the monsoon will bring us vessels, which come to be laden with ivory; on one of which you may obtain a passage."

The ships at length arrived; and my master, having chosen the one in which I was to embark, loaded it with ivory, making over half the cargo to me, which I ultimately sold for a large sum.

Arriving at Baghdad without any further adventures, I immediately presented myself to the Caliph, who told me that my long absence had occasioned him some uneasiness, which made him the more delighted to see me return in safety.

He bestowed more presents and honours upon me; after which I retired to my own home in this my native city of Baghdad, which I have not since quitted, and where I hope to end my days.

Sindbad thus concluded the recital of his seventh and last voyage; and, addressing himself to Hindbad, added : " Well, my friend, have you ever heard of one who has suffered more than I have, or been in so many trying situations ? Is it not just that after so many troubles I should enjoy an agreeable and quiet life? "

Hindbad · kissed his hand, and said : " I must confess that you have encountered frightful perils. You not only deserve a quiet life, but are worthy of all the riches you possess, since you make so good a use of them ! "

Sindbad caused Hindbad to receive another hundred pieces of gold ; in addition to which he continued to show him so much kindness that Hindbad, who had now no need to follow his late calling, for the remainder of his days had every reason to bless the name of Sindbad the Sailor.

ALADDIN: OR THE WONDERFUL LAMP.

IN the capital of one of the richest and most extensive provinces of China lived a poor, hardworking tailor whose name was Mustapha, together with his wife and his only son, Aladdin.

When the youth was old enough to learn a trade, his father took him to his shop, and began to show him how to use his needle. But no sooner was Mustapha's back turned than Aladdin, who was of an idle and careless disposition, was off, and returned no more during the day. His father frequently punished him, but Aladdin did not reform; and with great sorrow Mustapha was obliged at last to abandon him to his idle course, which he continued until his father's death.

As Aladdin's mother saw that her son would never follow the trade of his father, she shut up Mustapha's shop, and sold off all his stock, while Aladdin gave himself completely to idleness.

One day, when he was about fifteen, as he played with his companions in one of the public places, a stranger who was passing stopped and looked attentively at him.

Whether this stranger, who was a powerful magician, thought he saw in the face of Aladdin signs of a disposition well suited to his purpose is uncertain; but he very cleverly obtained information concerning Aladdin's family, and ascertained the sort of character and disposition he possessed, after which he went up to the youngster, and, taking him aside, asked him if his father was not called Mustapha, and whether he was not a tailor by trade.

" Yes, sir," replied Aladdin ; " but he has been dead a long time."

On hearing this, the Magician threw his arms round Aladdin's neck, and embraced him, while tears ran from his eyes. " Alas ! " he exclaimed, " I am your uncle ; your father was my most excellent brother, whom for years I have longed to meet once more. This is, indeed, sad news."

He then asked Aladdin where his mother lived, and when Aladdin had informed him, the Magician gave him a handful of small money, saying : " My son, go to your mother, make my respects to her, and tell her I will come and see her to-morrow."

H

Aladdin ran to his mother, highly delighted with the money that had been given him. " Pray tell me, mother," he cried, as he entered the house, " whether I have an uncle ? "

" No, my child," replied she, " you have no uncle, either on your poor father's side or on mine."

" For all that," answered the boy, " I have just seen a man who told me he was my father's brother and my uncle. He even wept and embraced me when I told him of my father's death. And to prove that he spoke the truth," added he, showing the money he had received, " see what he has given me ! He bade me also be sure and give his kindest greeting to you, and to say that he would come and see you to-morrow."

" It is true, indeed, my son," replied Aladdin's mother, " that your father had a brother once ; but, to the best of my belief, he has been dead a long time."

The next day the Magician again accosted Aladdin while he was playing with three other boys, and, putting two pieces of gold in his hand, said : " Take this, my boy, to your mother. Tell her I intend to come and sup with her this evening, and that I send this money that she may purchase what is necessary."

Aladdin carried home the two pieces of gold to his mother, who laid them out to the best advantage. When everything was ready, she desired Aladdin to go out into the street and look for his uncle. But before the boy could obey, there was a knock. Aladdin instantly opened the door, and saw the Magician, who had several bottles of wine in his hands, to add to the other good things his money had provided.

When the Magician had paid his respects to Aladdin's mother, he seated himself, and observed: " Do not be surprised, my good sister, that you have never seen me during the whole time you have been married to my late brother, Mustapha. It is full forty years since I left this country, and since then I have travelled nearly all over the world."

He then turned to Aladdin and asked: " What is your occupation ? Have you learned any trade ? "

But his mother answered for him. " Aladdin," she said, " is a very idle boy. His father did all he could to make him learn his business, but could not get him to work ; and since his death, Aladdin will learn nothing, but leads an absolutely idle life. Though I pass the whole day in spinning cotton, I can hardly get bread for us to eat," and she burst into tears.

" This is not right, Aladdin," said the Magician. " Dear nephew, you must think of supporting yourself, and working for your bread. If you have any objection to learning a trade, I will procure you a shop, and furnish it. You shall sell the goods, and with the profits that you make you shall buy other merchandise; and in this manner you will pass your life in ease and prosperity. Consult your own inclinations, and tell me candidly what you think of the plan."

This offer greatly flattered the vanity of Aladdin. He therefore admitted to the Magician that he thought favourably of the suggestion. " Very well," replied the Magician, " I will take you to-morrow and have you properly fitted out; and then we will look about for a shop of the description I have named."

Aladdin's mother, who till now had not been convinced that the Magician was really the brother of her husband, no longer doubted when she heard of the good he proposed to do her son. She thanked him sincerely for his kind intentions; and during supper charged Aladdin to prove himself worthy of the good fortune in store for him.

The Magician returned the next morning, according to promise. He took Aladdin to a merchant's where ready-made clothes of every description were sold, and made him try on several suits, saying: "Dear nephew, choose such as please you best."

When Aladdin saw himself handsomely dressed for the first time in his life, he overwhelmed his uncle with thanks, while his mother was transported with joy. "O generous relation," she exclaimed, "I thank you from the bottom of my heart. May you live many happy years."

"Aladdin," replied the Magician, "is not such a bad boy, after all. To-morrow I will call for him, and we will go sight-seeing. I have no doubt that we shall make him what we wish."

The next morning Aladdin got up very early in order to be ready to set out the moment his uncle called for him. Directly he saw the Magician coming, he went to inform his mother of the fact; then he took leave of her and ran to meet his uncle.

The Magician received Aladdin in the most affectionate manner. "Come," said he, with a smile, "I will to-day show you some very fine things." He then led the boy, who had never been outside the city, out at a gate, and showed him some magnificent palaces with beautiful gardens—gradually drawing him on and on until they had left the city far behind.

Aladdin, who had never in his life before taken

so long a walk, began to feel tired. "Where are we going, my dear uncle?" he asked. "I can see nothing but hills and mountains before us."

"Take courage, nephew," replied his pretended uncle; "I wish to show you something that far surpasses in magnificence all you have hitherto seen."

At length, they came to a narrow valley, situated between two mountains of nearly the same height. "We need go no farther," said the Magician. "I am now going to strike a light; and do you in the meantime collect all the dry sticks and leaves you can find, in order to make a fire."

Aladdin obeyed, and, as soon as the sticks blazed up, the Magician threw upon them a certain perfume. A thick and dense smoke immediately arose, the ground shook slightly, and, opening near the spot where they stood, disclosed a square stone of about a foot and a half across, with a brass ring fixed in the centre.

Aladdin, dreadfully alarmed, was about to run away, when the Magician stopped him. "Do not be afraid," he said, "I desire nothing of you but that you obey me implicitly. I must now inform you that under the stone which you see here is concealed a great treasure, which is destined for you, and which will one day render you richer than the most powerful monarchs of the earth. But, in order to insure success, you must observe and execute in every respect the instructions I am going to give you."

"What must I do?" asked Aladdin, overwhelmed with astonishment at what he had seen and heard. "Tell me; I am ready to obey you in everything."

"I heartily rejoice," replied the Magician, "that you have made so good a resolution. Come, then, take hold of this ring, and lift up the stone. It will come up without difficulty."

Aladdin did as the Magician told him; he raised the stone without any trouble, and laid it aside.

When the stone was taken away a hole was visible, at the bottom of which appeared a small door, with steps going still lower. "You must now, my boy," said the Magician to Aladdin, "observe exactly every direction I am going to give you. Go down into this cavern; and when you have come to the bottom of the steps, you will see an open door, which leads into three chambers opening out of each other, and which are full of gold and silver. But you must take particular care not to touch any of this treasure. At the end of the third chamber is a door which leads to a garden, planted with beautiful trees, all of which are laden with fruit. Go straight forward and follow a path which you will perceive, and which will bring you to a flight of fifty steps, at the top of which there is a terrace. When you have ascended to the terrace, you will observe a niche before you, in which there is a lighted lamp. Take the lamp, extinguish it, and bring it to me. If you should wish to gather any of the fruit in the garden you may do so."

Then the Magician took off a ring which he had on one of his fingers, and put it on Aladdin's hand, telling him that it would guard him against every evil that might happen. " Go," added he, "and descend boldly."

Aladdin jumped into the opening, and went down the steps. He found the three chambers and passed through them to the garden. Then, without stopping, he ascended to the terrace. He took the lamp which stood lighted in the niche, threw out its contents, and put it in his bosom. On his way back through the garden he stopped to look more carefully at the fruit, which he had only glanced at before. The fruit of each tree had a separate colour. Some were white, others sparkling and transparent ; some were red ; others green, blue, or violet ; some of a yellowish hue ; in short, there were fruits of almost every colour. The white were pearls; the sparkling and transparent fruits were diamonds; the deep red were rubies; the green emeralds; the blue turquoises; the violet amethysts; those tinged with yellow, sapphires. All were of the largest size, and the most perfect ever seen in the world, but Aladdin thought they were only pieces of coloured glass. Yet the variety and contrast of so many beautiful colours, as well as the brilliancy and great size of these fruits, tempted him to gather some of each kind; and he took so many of every colour, that he filled all his pockets, and stuffed others in his girdle and inside his shirt, until he had no room for more.

Laden in this manner, Aladdin made his way back to the entrance of the cave, where the Magician was impatiently waiting. As soon as Aladdin perceived him he called out: " Give me your hand, uncle, to help me up."

" My dear boy," replied the Magician, " you will do better first to give me the lamp."

" It is not at all in my way," said Aladdin, " I will give it you when I am out of the cave."

The Magician persisted in demanding the lamp before he would help Aladdin out of the cave; but the latter absolutely refused to give it up till he was out. The Magician then fell into the most violent rage. He muttered a spell, made some passes with his hands, and the stone which served to shut up the entrance to the cavern returned of its own accord to its place, the earth covering it exactly as when the Magician and Aladdin first arrived.

Now the Magician, who, of course, was *not* the uncle of Aladdin, had discovered by his magic that there was a wonderful lamp in a cave in the middle of China, the possession of which would make him the most powerful being in the universe, if he could succeed in laying hands on it. But it was absolutely necessary that another person should go down to take it, and then put it into his hands. For this reason he had addressed himself to Aladdin, who seemed to be an artless youth, well adapted to perform the service ; and he resolved, as soon as he had got the lamp from the boy, to sacrifice him so that no witness might exist who could say he was in possession of the lamp. But the event disappointed his hopes and expectations; for he was in such haste to sacrifice poor Aladdin that he defeated his own object.

When the Magician found all his hopes and expectations frustrated, there remained but one thing to do, and that was to return to Africa, his native country ; and this he did the very same day.

It might be supposed that Aladdin was now hopelessly lost ; indeed, the Magician himself, who thought he had destroyed the boy, had quite forgotten the ring he had placed on his finger ; but Aladdin, who, so far, knew not the wonderful qualities of either the ring or the lamp, was soon to be enlightened.

When he found himself thus buried alive, he called aloud a thousand times to his uncle, telling him he was ready to give up the lamp. But all his cries were useless, and, having no other means of making himself heard, he remained in darkness, bemoaning his un-happy fate. At last, he descended the steps and groped along the walls to the right and left several times, but could not discover the smallest opening. Finally, he sat down on the steps of his dungeon, without the least hope that he would ever again see the light of day.

Aladdin remained two days in this hopeless state. Then, regarding his death as certain, he lifted his hands, and joining them as in the act of prayer, wholly resigned himself to the will of Heaven. In this act of joining his hands he happened to rub the ring which the Magician had put upon his finger. Instantly, a Genie of enormous stature and a most horrid countenance rose, as it were, out of the earth before him. This

Genie was so tall that his head touched the vaulted roof, and he said to Aladdin: " What dost thou command ? I am ready to obey thee as thy slave—and the slave of all who have the ring that is on thy finger."

On any other occasion Aladdin would have been struck dumb with terror at sight of this startling figure ; but he was so taken up with the danger and peril of his situation that he answered without hesitation, " Whoever you are, take me, if you can, out of this place."

He had scarcely said the words when the earth opened, and he found himself outside the cave, at the very spot to which the Magician had brought him.

Looking round, he descried the city in the distance; but he was so faint and weak it was only with great difficulty that he got home. His mother, who already mourned him as lost or dead, was overcome by joy at sight of him.

But Aladdin begged for food, which he had the sense to eat slowly, while he drank with equal moderation. When he had done, he related to his mother all that had happened. He took the lamp out of his bosom and showed it to her, as well as the transparent and many-coloured fruits that he had gathered as he returned.

Aladdin had no sooner concluded the recital

of his adventures than his mother began to abuse the pretended uncle in the strongest terms. She called him a traitor, an assassin, and all the other names she could think of—embracing her son, and giving thanks for his deliverance.

Aladdin slept profoundly all night and, on rising, asked for breakfast. " Alas ! my son," replied his mother, " I have not a morsel of bread to give you. Last night you finished all there was in the house. But have patience. I have here a little cotton I have spun ; I will go and sell it, and purchase something for our dinner."

" Keep that for another time," said Aladdin, " and give me the lamp I brought yesterday. I will go and sell that ; the money it will bring will serve us for breakfast and dinner too— nay, perhaps, also for supper."

Aladdin's mother took the lamp from the place where she had placed it. " It seems to me to be very dirty," she said. " If I were to clean it a little perhaps it might sell for more."

She then took some water and a little fine sand to clean the lamp; but she had scarcely begun to rub when a hideous and gigantic Genie rose out of the ground before her, and cried with a voice as loud as thunder : " What are thy commands ? I am ready to obey thee as thy slave." The poor woman was so alarmed at this frightful apparition that she fell down in a fainting-fit.

But Aladdin had seen a similar appearance in the cavern; consequently, he did not lose his presence of mind, but seized the lamp, and answered firmly: " Bring me something to eat."

The Genie disappeared, returning a moment after with a large silver basin, which he carried on his head, and twelve covered dishes of the same material filled with the choicest meats; together with six loaves, two bottles of the most excellent wine, and some silver plates and cups. He placed all these things upon the ground and instantly vanished.

All this had occurred so quickly that Aladdin's mother had hardly recovered from her fainting-fit before the Genie had disappeared the second time.

On coming to her senses, she was astonished to see the large basin, the twelve dishes, the six loaves, the two bottles of wine, and other articles. " O, my son!" she cried, "how came this abundance here? "

" My good mother," replied Aladdin, " come, sit down, and eat. I will tell you everything when we have broken our fast."

When they had made an end of their meal and Aladdin's mother had taken away the things, and put aside what had not been consumed, she came and seated herself near her son.

" Why ? " she asked, " did the terrible being not rather address himself to you, to whom he had before appeared in the underground cavern ? "

" Mother," replied Aladdin, " the Genie who appeared just now to you is not the one who appeared to me. The Genie who came to you was the slave of the lamp you had in your hand."

" What ! " cried his mother, " was your lamp the reason why this terrible being addressed himself to me rather than to you ? Then take it out of my sight. Indeed, I would rather you should throw away or sell it than that I should run the risk of being killed with fright by again touching it. And, if you will follow my advice, you will put away the ring as well."

" With your permission, my dear mother," replied Aladdin, " I shall beware of parting with this lamp. Since chance has discovered its virtues to us, let us avail ourselves of them. But we must be careful not to make any parade of our new riches lest we draw upon ourselves the envy of our neighbours. I will take the lamp out of your sight, and put it where I shall be able to find it whenever I have occasion for it. Again, I cannot make up my mind to throw away the ring, but for which you would never have seen me again."

As the arguments of Aladdin appeared reasonable, his mother had no further objections to make.

The following morning, Aladdin took one of the silver plates, and went out early in order to sell it. He addressed himself to a Jew he happened to meet and, taking him aside, showed him the plate, and asked if he would buy it.

The Jew, a clever and cunning man, took the plate and examined it. Directly he had satisfied himself that it was good silver, he took out of his purse a piece of gold, which was exactly one seventy-second part of the value of the plate, and offered it to Aladdin, who accepted it eagerly.

He and his mother continued to live quietly and economically till Aladdin had sold all the twelve dishes, one after the other. When the money for the last plate was spent, Aladdin took the basin, which was at least ten times as heavy as any of the plates. For this the Jew counted out ten pieces of gold, with which Aladdin was satisfied.

When his ten pieces of gold were spent Aladdin

had recourse to the lamp. He took it and rubbed it, and the Genie whom he had before seen instantly appeared. But, as Aladdin had rubbed the lamp more gently than his mother had done, the Genie spoke to him in a softened tone.

"What are thy commands?" said he.

"I am hungry," cried Aladdin; "bring me something to eat."

The Genie disappeared, and in a short time returned, loaded as before, and again vanished.

When Aladdin again found his provisions gone, he took one of the new silver dishes, and went to look for the Jew who had bought the others from him. As he walked along, he happened to pass the shop of a goldsmith, a respectable and honest old man, who called him into the shop.

"My son," said he, "I have often seen you pass this way, loaded as you are now, and each time you have spoken to a certain Jew; and then I have seen you go back empty-handed. Perhaps you do not know that this Jew is a great cheat, and that no one who knows him will have any dealings with him? Now, if you will show me what you are carrying, and you wish to sell it, I will faithfully give you what it is worth, if it be in my way of business."

ɪ

Aladdin was only too pleased to agree to this; whereupon the old man, who knew at a glance that the plate was of the finest silver, took his scales, weighed the dish, and declared it to be worth seventy-two pieces of gold, which he immediately counted out.

Aladdin thanked the goldsmith, and for the future carried his dishes to no one else.

Although Aladdin and his mother had an inexhaustible source of money in their lamp, they continued to live with the same frugality they had always shown. Thus, mother and son passed their time happily together for several years, with the profitable assistance Aladdin occasionally procured from the lamp.

During this interval, Aladdin made acquaintance with some of the most considerable merchants of the town, and gradually acquired the style and manners of the company he kept. By frequenting the jewellers' shops he also learnt that the fruits he had gathered in the garden, and had taken to be only coloured glass, were jewels of enormous price.

One day, as he was walking abroad, Aladdin heard the criers reading a proclamation of the Sultan, ordering all persons to shut up their shops, and retire into their houses, until his daughter, the Princess Badroulboudour (a name which means " The Full Moon among Full Moons ") had passed on her way to the bath, and had returned to the palace.

Hearing this order created in Aladdin a curiosity to see the Princess. So he went and hid behind the door of the bath. He had not waited long before the Princess made her appearance, accompanied by a great crowd of women and servants. When she had come within three or four paces of the door she lifted the veil which had concealed her face, and thus gave Aladdin the opportunity he desired.

Till this moment Aladdin had never seen any woman without her veil, except his mother, who was rather old, and who, even in her youth, had not possessed any beauty. The appearance of the Princess dispelled the notion he had entertained that all women resembled his mother. She was, in fact, the most exquisite and charming creature imaginable; and it is not surprising that he was absolutely entranced by such loveliness.

When he came home, Aladdin was unable to conceal his state of mind from the observation of his mother. She asked if anything had happened to him, or if he were unwell. He gave her no answer whatever; but continued to brood upon the lovely image of the Princess Badroulboudour.

Aladdin passed a wakeful night; and the next morning he said to his mother: "You may not have heard that the Princess Badroulboudour, the daughter of our Sultan, went to the bath after dinner yesterday. I had the supreme happiness and satisfaction of seeing her; and this, my dear mother, is the true cause of the state you saw me in yesterday, and the reason of the silence I have hitherto kept. I feel such a violent affection for the Princess that I can never know a moment's happiness until she is my wife."

Aladdin's mother listened with great attention till he came to the last sentence, when she burst into a fit of laughter.

"Alas! my son," she cried, "you must surely have lost your senses to talk thus."

"Dear mother," replied Aladdin, "I foresaw very well that you would reproach me with folly and madness; but nothing will prevent me from again declaring my resolution to demand the Princess Badroulboudour of the Sultan in marriage."

"In truth, my son," replied his mother, very seriously, "you seem to have forgotten who you are; and even if you are determined to put this resolution in practice, I do not know who will have the boldness to carry your message to the Sultan."

"You, yourself, must do that," he answered.

"I!" cried his mother in amazement. "I go to the Sultan!—not I, indeed. Nothing shall induce me to engage in such an act of folly."

"My dear mother," replied Aladdin, "neither your reasons nor your remonstrances will in the least change my resolution. I have told you that I intend to demand the Princess Badroulboudour in marriage, and that you must impart my wish to the Sultan. I beg you not to refuse me this favour."

"My dear son," she replied, "I am your mother, and I am ready to do anything that is reasonable. But you, regardless of the lowness of your birth, demand nothing less than the daughter of your sovereign. Now, suppose I have the impudence to present myself before his Majesty, and make such a request; do you not see that I should be treated as a madwoman? And there is another reason, my son; no one ever appears before the Sultan without offering him some present when a favour is sought at his hands. What present have you to offer?"

Aladdin listened with the greatest patience and answered :

" You say it is not customary to request an audience of the Sultan without carrying a present in your hand. I agree with you. But, when you tell me I have nothing worthy of his acceptance, you forget those things we thought were pieces of coloured glass. I know their value better now, and can inform you that they are precious stones of priceless worth, and worthy of the acceptance of a great sovereign."

In the end, Aladdin's mother gave way to her son's arguments; and early the next day, a selection of the jewels having been made and arranged in a porcelain dish, which was then wrapped in a fine linen cloth, she took the road towards the palace of the Sultan. But, though she succeeded in gaining admission with the rest of the crowd to the Hall of Audience, where the monarch in person heard petitions and administered justice, she returned home, much to Aladdin's disappointment, without having ventured to approach the Sultan.

For several days in succession did the good woman resort to the palace, bearing her offering of jewels, without finding any opportunity of carrying out her mission. On the sixth day, however, the Sultan, on retiring to his apartment, said to his Grand Vizier : " For some time past I have observed a certain woman who comes regularly every day when I hold my council, and who carries something in her hand wrapped in a linen cloth. The next day the council sits, if she returns, do not fail to call her, that I may hear what she has to say."

The mother of Aladdin returned to the palace the next day the council met, and placed herself opposite the Sultan, who, touched by her patience and perseverance, said to the Grand Vizier, " Do you observe the woman I mentioned to you the other day ? Order her to come here, and we will begin by hearing what she has to say."

The Grand Vizier immediately pointed out the woman in question to the chief of the ushers, who signed to the mother of Aladdin to approach. She obeyed, and prostrated herself until the Sultan commanded her to rise, saying : " What is the business which brings you here day after day, my good woman ? "

Aladdin's mother answered : " Oh, gracious monarch, I entreat you to pardon the boldness of the request I am about to make, which is of a most private nature." The Sultan, having commanded all to withdraw but the Grand Vizier, told her she might speak, and exhorted her to tell the truth without fear.

Aladdin's mother then faithfully related to

the Sultan by what means Aladdin had seen the Princess Badroulboudour, and with what a violent passion the sight of the Princess had inspired him; concluding by imploring his pardon for herself and her son, who had dared to dream of so illustrious an alliance.

The Sultan listened to this speech with the greatest patience. Before he returned any answer, he asked what it was she had with her tied up in a cloth. Upon this, Aladdin's mother took up the porcelain dish, which she had set down at the foot of the throne. Removing the linen cloth, she presented the dish to the Sultan.

It is impossible to express the astonishment of the monarch when he beheld in the dish such a quantity of the most precious, perfect, and brilliant jewels—greater in size and value than any he had ever seen. After admiring the jewels separately, he turned to his Grand Vizier, and said: "What do you say to such a present? Is not the donor worthy of the Princess, my daughter?"

Now the Grand Vizier had entertained great hopes of the Sultan making a match between the Princess and his own son; therefore he replied:

"Everyone must allow that this present is not unworthy of the Princess. All the same, as the young man is a complete stranger, I beg your Majesty to make some excuse to put off the marriage for three months."

The Sultan, who was an easy-going monarch, agreed to this. "Return home," he said to Aladdin's mother, "and tell your son that I consent to the proposal he has made through you; but the preparations for my daughter's marriage will take three months. At the end of that time you may return."

As soon as Aladdin saw his mother's face he knew that she had good tidings. And when she had told him all, he thought himself the happiest and most fortunate of mortals—though the three months would seem like three years, he declared.

It happened one evening, when about two months of the time had gone, that Aladdin's mother found she had no oil in the house. Accordingly, she went out to see if she could get some ; and on going into the city perceived signs of great festivity and rejoicing. All the shops, instead of being shut, were open, and ornamented with green branches and other decorations ; and preparations were evidently being made for an illumination. Aladdin's mother asked the oil merchant what it all meant. "Where do you come from, good woman," said he, "that you do not know that the son of the Grand Vizier is this evening to be married to the Princess Badroulboudour ? "

Aladdin's mother did not wait to hear more, but returned home with all possible speed.

" All is lost, my son ! " she exclaimed. "This very evening the son of the Grand Vizier is to marry the Princess Badroulboudour at the palace."

This news came upon Aladdin like a thunder-clap. Then he bethought himself of the lamp, and, retiring to his room, he took it from its hiding-place and rubbed it. The Genie instantly appeared.

" What are thy commands ? " said he to Aladdin.

" Attend to me," answered Aladdin : " I have now a business of great importance for you to undertake. The Sultan promised me the hand of his daughter; but he has, instead, given her in marriage to the son of his Grand Vizier. What I order you to do is this : as soon as the bride and bridegroom have retired to rest, take them up and instantly bring them both here."

" Oh, master," replied the Genie, "I will obey thee," and immediately disappeared.

In the meantime every preparation was made in the Sultan's palace to celebrate the nuptials of the Princess ; and the whole evening was spent in ceremonies and rejoicings until the time came for retiring.

But the bridegroom had scarcely laid his head upon the pillow when the faithful slave of the lamp took up the bed with the bride and bridegroom in it; and, to the great astonishment of them both, in an instant transported them to Aladdin's chamber, where he set them down.

Aladdin then ordered him to take the bridegroom and shut him up in the lumber-room, and to return at daybreak. The Genie obeyed. He also improved on Aladdin's orders by breathing on the unfortunate young man and rendering him incapable of movement. Then Aladdin addressed himself to the Princess, explaining that what had been done was simply to prevent the Sultan from marrying his daughter to another after he had promised her to Aladdin. But the Princess was so alarmed at this extraordinary adventure that Aladdin could not get a word out of her. So he laid himself down in the place of the Grand Vizier's son, with his back turned towards the Princess, having first placed a drawn sabre between the lady and himself.

Punctually next morning the Genie appeared and, releasing the bridegroom from his uncomfortable position, carried him and the bride back to the palace—the Genie in all these operations being visible only to Aladdin.

Both the Sultan and the Sultana visited their daughter in the course of the morning, and were surprised to find her looking very upset. To the inquiries of the former she would answer nothing; but to her mother the Princess related how, on the previous night, the bed had been taken up and transported into an ill-furnished and dismal chamber, where she was separated from her husband, whose place was then taken by a complete stranger; and that, when morning approached, her husband was restored to her, and they were both brought back again to the palace in a single instant.

The Sultana listened with great attention; but she could not give credit to her daughter's story.

"You have done well, my child," she said to the Princess, "not to inform the Sultan, your father, of this matter. Take care that you mention it to no one, unless you wish to be considered a madwoman."

She then ordered the son of the Grand Vizier to be called, in order to question him about what the Princess had told her. But the young man felt himself so highly honoured by this alliance with the Sultan, that he pretended to be unaware that anything unusual had happened.

The next night, at the same time, Aladdin again summoned the Genie, with the result that the bride and bridegroom were again whisked off, and everything happened precisely as before. But this repetition of her amazing experience so terrified the Princess, that this time she herself informed the Sultan of all that had happened.

The Sultan sympathized fully with the distress this surprising adventure must have excited in his daughter's mind. " My child," said he, " you were wrong not to divulge to me yesterday the strange story you have just related. I have not bestowed you in marriage to render you unhappy. Banish from your memory, then, what you have been telling me : I will take care that you shall experience no more such nights as those which you have suffered."

He then sent for the Grand Vizier, whose son had also related his alarming and uncomfortable experiences ; and who now informed his father that, in spite of the honour he derived from his exalted alliance with the daughter of his sovereign, he would rather die than have to undergo any more adventures of the kind. Consequently, when the Sultan spoke to the

Grand Vizier of annulling the marriage he made no objection; and this was accordingly done.

Aladdin, though overjoyed, was not surprised when the news reached him. He allowed the remainder of the three months to elapse, and then again sent his mother to the palace, to put the Sultan in mind of his promise. This time she was bolder, and, advancing to the foot of the throne without hesitation, prostrated herself in the usual manner. After she had risen, the Sultan asked her what she wished.

"O mighty monarch," she replied, "I again present myself before the throne of your Majesty to announce to you, in the name of my son Aladdin, that the three months during which you desired him to wait have expired."

When, on the former occasion, the Sultan had desired a delay of three months before he acceded to the request of this good woman, he thought he would hear no more of a marriage which appeared to him entirely unsuited to the Princess; for he naturally judged of the suitor's position from the humble appearance of Aladdin's mother.

He therefore consulted in a low tone with the Grand Vizier, who said: "It seems to me that there is a very easy method to avoid this unequal marriage. It is to set so high a price upon the Princess, your daughter, that all this suitor's riches, however great they may be, cannot provide it."

The Sultan approved of this advice, and, after some little reflection, said to Aladdin's mother : " Good woman, I am ready to render your son happy by uniting him to the Princess, my daughter ; but, as I cannot bestow her in marriage till I have seen proofs that she will be well provided for, tell your son that I will fulfil my promise as soon as he sends me forty large basins of massive gold, full of jewels like those you have already presented from him. These basins must be carried by forty black slaves, each of whom shall be accompanied by a white slave, young, handsome, and richly dressed. Go, my good woman, and I will wait till you bring me his answer."

Aladdin's mother again prostrated herself at the foot of the throne, and returned home, where she gave her son an exact account of everything the Sultan had said, and of the conditions upon which he consented to the marriage.

Aladdin replied : " What he requires of me is a trifle in comparison with what I would give to possess such a treasure as the Princess. Will you go and prepare dinner, and leave me awhile to myself ? "

As soon as his mother had gone, Aladdin took the lamp and rubbed it. The Genie instantly appeared, and demanded to know what was required of him.

" The Sultan agrees to give me the Princess, his daughter, in marriage," said Aladdin ; " but he demands of me forty large basins of massive gold, filled with jewels. He requires, also, that these forty basins should be brought to him by forty black slaves, accompanied by an equal number of young and handsome white slaves, richly dressed. Go and procure me all this as soon as possible."

In a short time, the Genie returned with forty black slaves, each carrying upon his head a large golden basin of great weight, full of pearls, diamonds, rubies, and emeralds. They were accompanied by forty white slaves. On Aladdin expressing his satisfaction, the Genie disappeared.

Aladdin's mother now returned from market ; and great was her surprise at the sight which met her eyes. But, before she could speak, she was told she must at once return to the palace, and deliver to the Sultan the dowry he had demanded.

As this marvellous procession of black and

white slaves, all gorgeously arrayed and laden with jewels, and followed by the mother of Aladdin, passed through the streets the people came running from all sides.

On the arrival of the slaves at the palace, the porters bowed to the ground, thinking they must be the retinue of some great prince. The Sultan, informed of what was happening, ordered the doors to be thrown open, and the whole party, prostrating themselves in a semi-circle, placed the jewels on the ground at the foot of the throne, while the mother of Aladdin thus addressed the monarch : " O mighty ruler, my son, Aladdin, is well aware that the present he has sent your Majesty is much beneath the inestimable worth of the Princess Badroulboudour. He, nevertheless, hopes that your Majesty will graciously accept it and that it may find favour in the eyes of the Princess."

The Sultan hesitated no longer. The mere sight of such immense riches, and the wonderful speed with which Aladdin had fulfilled his exorbitant request, without making the least difficulty, persuaded him that Aladdin must be a desirable son-in-law.

" Go, my good woman," he said, his eyes fixed greedily upon all this splendour, " and tell your son I am waiting with open arms to receive and embrace him ; and that the greater diligence he uses in coming to receive from my hands the gift I am ready to bestow upon him, in the person of my daughter, the greater pleasure he will afford me."

The mother of Aladdin returned home swelling with pride and happiness. " You have every reason, my dear son," she said, " to be satisfied. The Sultan has announced that you are worthy to possess the Princess Badroulboudour, and he is now waiting to embrace you and to conclude the marriage."

Aladdin was delighted at this intelligence, and instantly retired to his chamber. He then took up the lamp, rubbed it, and immediately the Genie showed his ready obedience to its power by appearing in readiness to execute his commands.

" Oh, Genie," said Aladdin to him, " I now desire thee to provide me with a richer and more magnificent dress than was ever worn by any monarch."

This was a very simple matter for the Genie; and the dress in which he now assisted Aladdin to array himself was so dazzling that it made the eyes of the beholder ache. He also provided him with a horse with jewelled harness and saddle, and forty more slaves, in addition to ten thousand pieces of gold to distribute to the crowd.

Aladdin's mother was not forgotten ; for her dutiful son presented her with six magnificent dresses and as many female attendants.

Aladdin then mounted his horse, and began his triumphal progress through the streets, scattering handfuls of gold among the throng which pressed around him.

So he came to the palace, where the Sultan was so favourably impressed and agreeably surprised by his first sight of his new and unknown son-in-law that he descended three steps of his throne to prevent Aladdin from throwing himself at his feet, and embraced him with the most evident marks of affection.

After some polite speeches had passed between them, the Sultan conducted Aladdin to a magnificent saloon, where a great feast had been prepared. The Sultan and Aladdin sat together, waited upon by the Grand Vizier and the nobles of the court; after which the Sultan ordered the chief judge to attend, and commanded him to draw up a contract of marriage between the Princess Badroulboudour and Aladdin.

When the judge had drawn up the contract with all the requisite forms, the Sultan asked Aladdin if he wished to remain in the palace and to conclude the ceremonies that day.

"O mighty monarch," he replied, "I request you to permit me to defer my happiness until I have built a palace for the Princess that shall be worthy even of her merit and dignity. And I entreat your Majesty to have the goodness to point out a suitable situation. I will then neglect nothing to get it finished with all possible diligence."

"My son," answered the Sultan, "there is a large open space in front of my palace which I shall be delighted to let you have for the purpose." With these kind words he again embraced Aladdin.

The young man then took leave of the Sultan and returned home in the same order in which he had come, receiving acclamations from the people, who wished him all happiness and prosperity. Retiring to his room, he instantly rubbed the lamp, and summoned the Genie.

"Oh, Genie," said Aladdin, "I have hitherto had every reason to praise the precision and promptitude with which thou hast executed whatever I have required. I now command thee to build me a palace as quickly as possible, opposite to that belonging to the Sultan, and at a short distance from it; and let this palace be in every way worthy to receive the Princess Badroulboudour, my bride. I leave the choice of the materials and the design to thee. But on the top floor let there be a large chamber with four walls of gold and silver; and let there be six windows in each wall, twenty-three of which have their frames set with jewels of the first water. I wish this palace to have a large court in the front, another at the back, and a garden. Above all, be sure that there is a room well filled with money, both gold and silver. Stables I must likewise have, filled with the most beautiful horses; also grooms and attendants; and female slaves for the service of the Princess. Go, and return as soon as thy task is completed."

The sun had already gone down when Aladdin had finished giving his orders to the Genie respecting the construction of the palace. The very next morning, when day broke, Aladdin had scarcely risen before the Genie presented himself.

" O master," said he, " thy palace is finished. Come, and see if it is to thy liking."

The Genie transported him there in an instant; and when Aladdin had examined the whole palace, which exceeded his utmost expectations, and had seen all the riches and magnificence it contained, he exclaimed : " O Genie, no one can be more satisfied than I. There is one thing only which I did not mention to thee; it is, to have a carpet of the finest velvet laid from the gate of the Sultan's palace to the door of the apartment which is reserved for the Princess."

" I will return in an instant," replied the Genie; and he had not been gone a moment before Aladdin saw the carpet he had ordered rolled out by invisible hands. The Genie then carried Aladdin back to his own house.

The Sultan's porters, who came to open the gates, and who were accustomed to see an open space where Aladdin's palace now stood, were much astonished at observing that space occupied by a new and magnificent building, and at seeing a lovely velvet carpet, which seemed to stretch from its gateway to that of the Sultan's abode. The news of this wonder soon spread through the palace; and the Grand Vizier was no less astonished than were the rest. The first thing he did was to go to the Sultan; but he tried to represent the whole business as enchantment. The Sultan, however, replied: " After the display of riches we have seen, can you think it so extraordinary that my son-in-law should be able to build a palace in this short time? He wished, no doubt, to surprise us;

and we every day see what miracles riches can perform."

When Aladdin had returned home and dismissed the Genie, he found that his mother was up, and had begun to put on one of the magnificent dresses he had ordered for her the day before, and in which she admired herself immensely. When her toilet was completed she proceeded to the palace, in order to wait upon her new daughter-in-law. Aladdin then mounted his horse, and left his paternal house, never more to return ; but he did not forget to take with him his wonderful lamp, which had been the cause of all his happiness and prosperity.

Aladdin's mother was received with great honour, and was taken by the chief steward to the apartment of the Princess Badroulboudour, who ran and embraced her, and made her sit upon her own couch. The Sultan also paid her great honour and respect, being much struck, after her former humble appearance, at finding her as magnificently attired as the Princess, his daughter.

When evening approached, the Princess took leave of the Sultan, her father, and began her progress to her new dwelling, with Aladdin's mother on her left hand, followed by a hundred female slaves, all magnificently dressed, and accompanied by bands of music and four hundred pages carrying torches.

In this order did the Princess proceed, walking upon the carpet which extended from Aladdin's palace to that of the Sultan, until she arrived at her destination, where Aladdin ran, with every expression of joy, to welcome her.

" O adorable Princess," he cried, " if I should have had the misfortune to displease you by my boldness in aspiring to an alliance with the daughter of my Sultan, please to consider that it was to your beautiful eyes and to your charms alone that you must attribute my rashness."

" O Prince, for thus I must now call you," replied the Princess, " I obey the will of the Sultan, my father ; and now that I have seen you, I freely own that I obey him without reluctance."

Aladdin was delighted at this charming answer. He kissed the Princess's hand, and then conducted her into a large saloon where there was a table spread with everything rare and delicious, and where all the dishes, cups and other articles were of solid gold.

The Princess Badroulboudour, Aladdin, and his mother sat down to table, where, as they feasted, they were entertained by a concert provided by invisible performers, arranged by the Genie.

It was nearly midnight when, according to the custom at that time observed in China, Aladdin rose and presented his hand to the Princess Badroulboudour, that they might dance together, and thus finish the ceremony of their nuptials.

The next morning Aladdin went to his father-in-law's palace and begged him to do him the honour of taking breakfast with him.

The Sultan readily granted this request, as he was anxious to see the inside of the palace of Aladdin. He was much struck by the beauty of the exterior; but his expressions of surprise and pleasure grew louder and higher as he passed from room to room ; and when he came to the chamber with the twenty-three jewelled case-ments he was so much astonished that he stood absolutely still.

" Nowhere," he exclaimed, " will anything be found to equal this. This palace is one of the wonders of the world. There is, however, one thing at which I am astonished, and that is, to observe that one of the windows is unfinished. Is it through forgetfulness, or neglect, or because the workmen have not had time to put the finishing strokes to this beautiful specimen of architecture ? "

" My Lord," answered Aladdin, " it is left unfinished on purpose, as I wish your Majesty to put the finishing-stroke to the palace, that I may thus have a memento of the favour I have received from you."

" If you have left it with that view," replied the Sultan, " I will give the necessary orders with the greatest pleasure. '

Aladdin then conducted him to the chamber where he had entertained the Princess Badroulboudour on the previous evening, and where two tables were set in the most magnificent manner. The Sultan sat at the first table, and ate with his daughter, Aladdin, and the Grand Vizier, while the rest of the court officials were regaled at the second table.

Now, although Aladdin had requested the Sultan to complete the twenty-fourth window in the gold and silver chamber, he knew that he would be unable to make it match the others. And it was so ; for, though the Sultan summoned the chief jewellers and goldsmiths in the kingdom, and furnished them with the finest of his jewels, they were only able to finish about half of it. Aladdin, therefore, not only made them stop working, but even undo all they had done and carry back the jewels to the Sultan.

Then he took out the lamp, rubbed it, and

ordered the Genie to complete the work. This the Genie did in the twinkling of an eye. So that when the Sultan—who had been much surprised at the report of the goldsmiths and jewellers, and the return of the jewels—came to inquire into the matter, he was still more amazed to find the work done.

" My dear son," he cried, in astonishment, " what a man you are, who can do such wonderful things almost instantly! There is not your equal in the world."

As time went on, Aladdin, by his kindness, courtesy and generosity, became beloved by all who came in contact with him. And so several happy years passed quickly by.

And now it is time to refer to one who, it may be thought, has passed right out of the story—and that is the Magician.

For some years he had remained in the belief that Aladdin had perished in the cavern in which he had imprisoned him. But about this time it occurred to him to make certain.

When, by means of his magic, he discovered that Aladdin was not only alive, but living in honour and splendour, he was greatly enraged —especially as he had no doubt that Aladdin owed all his good fortune to the lamp.

Therefore, the very next day, he started for China, with the intention of revenging himself.

He arrived at the city where Aladdin lived, and was soon in possession of most of the facts which have been related.

He visited and inspected the wonderful palace, and, filled with fury at this evidence of the fortune and greatness of Aladdin, he determined at all hazards to obtain possession of the lamp which had wrought these wonders.

His first object was to discover its whereabouts. His magic art soon informed him that the lamp was in Aladdin's palace, and his joy was so great on learning this that he could hardly contain himself. " I shall get this lamp," he cried, " and then I will fling the fellow back into that obscurity and poverty from which he has taken so high a leap."

It happened, most unfortunately for Aladdin, that just at this time he was absent on a hunting expedition, which was to last several days.

As soon as the Magician had discovered this, he went to the shop of a man who made and sold lamps.

" I want," said he, " a dozen copper lamps."

The man replied that he had not so many in his shop, but if his customer would wait till the next day he would have them ready for him, very well polished.

The next morning the Magician received the twelve lamps. He put them in a basket he had provided for the purpose, and went with this on his arm to the neighbourhood of Aladdin's palace. Here he walked to and fro, crying with a loud voice : " Who will exchange old lamps for new ones ? " All who passed laughed at his apparent folly. " That man," said they, " must surely have lost his senses, to offer to exchange new lamps for old."

The Magician was not surprised at the ridicule with which he was assailed. He seemed only intent on disposing of his merchandise, and continued to cry : " Who will exchange old lamps for new ? " He repeated this so often, as he walked to and fro on all sides of the palace, that at last the Princess Badroulboudour heard his voice, and sent one of her slaves to find out the reason of the noise and bustle.

The slave presently returned, laughing heartily. " O Princess," she said, " there is a fool outside with a basket on his arm full of beautiful new lamps, which he will not sell, but offers to exchange for old ones."

Another of the female slaves hereupon said : " There is an old lamp on a shelf in one of the chambers which seems to belong to no one. If the Princess will give me leave, I will try whether this fellow is really fool enough to give me a new lamp for an old one."

The Princess, who, unfortunately, was ignorant of the value of the lamp, which Aladdin usually kept locked up, consented, and sent the slave, who, beckoning to the Magician, said, "Give me a new lamp for this."

The Magician at once guessed that this was the very lamp he was seeking. He eagerly took it, and bade the slave choose which of the new ones she would have. She selected the brightest and biggest, and carried it to the Princess in triumph.

The Magician, having now no further use for his load of lamps, left his basket in a by-street, and made haste to find a retired spot outside the city. He then drew the lamp from his bosom, and rubbed it. The Genie instantly obeyed the summons. "What are thy commands?" cried the Genie.

"I command you," replied the Magician, "instantly to take the palace which you have erected in this city, and transport it, and me also, into Africa."

When the Sultan, on rising the next morning, looked out of the window and saw only an open space where the palace of Aladdin had stood, he thought at first he was dreaming, and rubbed his eyes. " I cannot be deceived," he said to himself ; " it was in this very place that I beheld it. If it had fallen, the materials would lie strewn around ; and if the earth had swallowed it, we should still see some signs of disturbance."

He sent in haste for the Grand Vizier. " Look out of the window," said the Sultan, on his arrival, " and tell me if you can see Aladdin's palace."

The Grand Vizier was as much amazed as the Sultan had been. When he was quite sure the palace of Aladdin had disappeared, he said ; " Your Majesty may remember that I declared, first of all, that this palace was the work of magic."

The Sultan, who could not deny this, was the more angry with Aladdin.

" Where is this impostor, this wretch ? " he exclaimed, " that I may strike off his head. Go, and order thirty of my horsemen to bring him before me in chains."

The horsemen set out, and met Aladdin, who was returning from the chase, about five or six leagues from the city.

" Prince Aladdin," said the officer in command, " it is with the greatest regret that I must inform you that we are sent to arrest you. We entreat you not to be angry with us for doing our duty."

This declaration astonished Aladdin beyond measure. He felt himself innocent, and asked the officer if he knew of what crime he was accused ; but the officer replied that neither he nor his men could give him any information.

Thereupon Aladdin dismounted and said : " I submit : execute whatever orders you have received."

When the guards entered the suburbs, all the people who saw Aladdin led in chains like a criminal felt sure he was going to lose his head. As he was generally beloved, some seized sabres, others whatever arms they could find, and those who had no weapons whatever took up stones, and tumultuously followed the guards.

Thus Aladdin was brought before the Sultan, who commanded the executioner, who was already present by his orders, to strike off his head.

But, at that critical instant, the Grand Vizier called the Sultan's attention to the fact that a great crowd had overcome the guards, and were preparing to storm the palace.

The Sultan was so alarmed at this that he ordered the executioner to sheath his sabre, to take the bandage off Aladdin's eyes, and set him at liberty.

When Aladdin found himself free he raised his hands in supplication, and entreated the Sultan to tell him for what crime he had just pardoned him. " Thy crime, perfidious wretch ! " exclaimed the Sultan. " Follow me, and I will show thee."

He led Aladdin to a window. " You know where your palace stood," he said. " Look around, and tell me what has become of it."

Aladdin looked, but saw nothing except the space which his palace had lately occupied.

" O mighty king," replied Aladdin, " I see it has disappeared ; but I can assure your Majesty that I had no share whatever in removing it."

" I care not what has become of your palace," replied the Sultan ; " I esteem my daughter a million times beyond that ; and unless you discover and bring her back to me, be assured your head shall answer for it."

" Great king," said Aladdin, " I entreat your Majesty to grant me forty days to make the most diligent inquiries ; and if I do not, within that period, succeed in my search, I will lay my head at the foot of your throne, that you may dispose of me according to your pleasure."

" I grant your request," answered the Sultan, rather reluctantly.

Aladdin left the Sultan's presence in the deepest distress and humiliation.

For three days he roamed about the city, eating only what was given him in charity, and unable to come to any decision.

At length, as he could not bear to remain longer in a place where he had lived in such splendour, he bent his steps towards the country. He came, towards the close of day, to the bank of a river. " Whither shall I go to seek my palace ? " he murmured to himself. " In what part of the world shall I find either my dwelling or my dear Princess ? " The bank was steep and slippery, and as he spoke, he slipped. Happy was it for him that he still had on his finger the ring the Magician had given him ; for, in grasping a projecting stone to save himself, he rubbed the ring, and the same Genie instantly appeared whom he had seen before in the underground cavern. " What are thy commands ? " cried the Genie.

Aladdin was most agreeably surprised by the sight of this unexpected help. He instantly replied : " Save my life, Genie, a second time, by transporting me to the spot where my palace is, and placing me under the window of the Princess Badroulboudour." So soon as he had said the words, the Genie took him up, and transported him to Africa, in the neighbourhood of a great city. In the midst of a large meadow in which the palace now stood, he set him down directly under the window of the Princess, and there left him.

As it was then night, Aladdin lay down under a tree to wait for daylight. Being now full of hope, he soon fell asleep.

The Princess Badroulboudour rose next morning much earlier than she had done since she had been transported to Africa by the artifice of the Magician, whose hated presence she was compelled to endure once every day. When she was dressed, one of her women, looking through the lattice, perceived Aladdin, who was gazing up, and instantly ran to tell her mistress the glad news. The Princess, who could scarcely believe the fact, immediately went to the window and herself saw him. She opened the lattice, and Aladdin greeted her with the greatest joy. "Lose not a moment!" cried the Princess; "they have gone to open the secret door."

This secret door was directly below the apartment of the Princess. Aladdin entered, and in another instant all their troubles were forgotten in the joy of meeting.

At length, Aladdin said: "Before you speak of anything else, my Princess, tell me what has become of that old lamp which I left upon a shelf before I went hunting?"

"Alas! my dear husband," replied the Princess, "I greatly fear our misfortunes are connected with that lamp; and what the more distresses me is that it was I who meddled with it."

She then gave Aladdin an account of all that had happened relative to the exchange of the old lamp for a new one. Then she told how, on the following night, she had felt the palace flying through the air, and had found herself next morning in Africa, a fact she had learnt from the Magician.

"O Princess," replied Aladdin, interrupting her, as she was again blaming herself for all that had occurred. "The fault was mine for not having left the lamp in security. But tell me, if you can, where he keeps it."

"He constantly carries it in his bosom," replied the Princess: "I am sure of this, because he once took it out in my presence, showing it as a sort of trophy when he was trying to persuade me to be faithless to you, and to take him for my husband. But he never had any answer from me save disdain."

"My Princess," interrupted Aladdin, "I trust I have discovered the means of delivering you from our enemy. For this purpose, however,

I must go into the town. Watch for my return."

Aladdin took the road that led to the town, and when he got there he went into a lane appropriated to druggists. Entering the best shop, he asked the owner if he could sell him a certain powder.

The merchant replied that he kept it, but that it was very dear. Aladdin therefore took out his purse, and purchased half a dram for a piece of gold. Returning to the palace, where the secret door was opened instantly, he informed the Princess of the plan he had arranged for her deliverance.

" You must," he said, attire yourself in one of your finest dresses, and when the Magician pays you a visit receive him with all the affability you can assume. Give him to understand that you are making the greatest efforts to forget me ; and, that he may be the more convinced of your sincerity, invite him to sup with you. But tell him that you have no wine fit for the occasion. On hearing this he will leave you to procure some. In his absence, you must put this powder into one of the cups. Then, upon the first opportunity, you must fill it with wine and induce him to drink it. Scarcely will he have emptied the cup when you will see him fall backwards."

The Princess promised to carry out these directions, and Aladdin took his leave.

As soon as he was gone, the Princess made her women dress her in the most becoming manner. She put on her richest attire, choosing those ornaments which set off her beauty to the greatest advantage; and when the Magician made his appearance at his usual hour, she rose to greet him in all the splendour of her beauty and her gorgeous array. She pointed to the most honourable seat, and, altogether, treated him with a civility she had never before shown him.

When he had taken his seat, the Princess looked at him with an air of kindness which made him suppose she no longer beheld him with aversion, and then said to him: "You are doubtless surprised at the change in me. But I have been thinking matters over and have decided that, as my father, in his rage, has doubtless put Aladdin to death, and as, therefore, an ocean of tears would be unavailing, I will shed no more, but make the best of things as they are. I, accordingly, begin by inviting you to supper. But as I have no wine worthy of the occasion, I must ask you to supply that yourself."

The Magician, who had never flattered himself that he should so soon and so easily acquire the good graces of the Princess, hastened to accept the invitation. " I will go and bring two bottles, and return immediately," he said.

" The longer you are gone, the more impatient shall I be to see you again," replied the Princess.

Delighted beyond measure, the Magician hastened to bring the wine, while the Princess threw the powder which Aladdin had given her into a goblet, and set it aside until she should call for it.

On the Magician's return they sat down to supper, the Princess paying every attention to her guest.

Then, having given one of her women the signal to fill with wine the cup she had prepared, she said : " In China, when two lovers drink together, they change goblets, and then drink to each other's health." With these words, she presented to her companion the goblet she held, and put out her other hand to receive his. The Magician hastened to make the exchange and, having drained the cup to the last drop, fell back dead in his chair.

The Princess then ordered one of her women to admit Aladdin, who opened the vest of the Magician, took out the lamp and rubbed it. The Genie instantly presented himself, and made his usual profession of service.

" Oh, Genie," said Aladdin, " I command you,

in the name of this lamp, to take this palace, and transport it to the same spot in China whence it was brought."

The Genie testified his obedience, and the journey was made immediately. Only two slight shocks were perceptible ; one, when the palace was taken up from the place where it stood in Africa, the other when it was set down in China, opposite to the Sultan's palace : and this was all the work of little more than an instant.

Since the disappearance of Aladdin's palace, and the loss of the Princess Badroulboudour, whom he did not hope to see again, the Sultan had been inconsolable. Every morning, as soon as he had risen, he went to look out of the window in the direction where the palace of Aladdin had stood. When, on the morning following the events just described, he found the space no longer empty, he could not believe his eyes. But when convinced that it was no delusion, his joy was so great that, without waiting for his attendants, he started off, and was received by Aladdin at the door of his palace.

" O Aladdin," cried the Sultan, " I cannot speak to you till I have embraced my dear daughter."

The Princess had just finished dressing when the Sultan entered. He eagerly embraced her, while the Princess, on her part, showed the greatest delight at again beholding him, and gave an exact account of all that had taken place from the moment the Magician had been heard crying, " New lamps for old ! " outside the palace.

At the conclusion of her story, the Sultan expressed his astonishment over and over again. Then, having again embraced Aladdin and his daughter, he returned to his palace and ordered a grand festival, to last ten days, to celebrate the occasion.

In due course the Sultan died, and the Princess came to the throne, sharing her power with Aladdin. They were beloved by everybody, and lived together happily for very many years.

THE ENCHANTED HORSE

ONCE upon a time there was a King of Persia named Sabur, who had one son and one daughter. The son, whose name was Feroze-shah, and who was the apple of his father's eye, was the handsomest, bravest, and most amiable Prince in all the world.

On the first day of the year, which was observed as a festival, the King was in the habit of holding a public audience, at which he received gifts and congratulations, and bestowed pardons and rewards.

On one of these occasions, a Hindu presented himself before the King with a horse made of ebony, inlaid with ivory. This horse was so well modelled that it almost seemed to be alive.

The King was delighted with its appearance, and at once offered to buy it.

But the Hindu, prostrating himself before the King, explained that this was an Enchanted Horse, which would carry the rider wherever he wished to go, in the shortest possible time. He added that he was willing to part with it on one condition only ; but, before stating that condition, he would give an exhibition of the creature's powers.

" Then mount," said the King, " and bring me a branch of the palm tree which grows at the foot of yonder hill." And he pointed to a hill about three leagues away.

The Hindu at once mounted, and, turning a peg on the right side of the horse's neck, was instantly borne upwards and carried through the air at a great height, and with the speed of lightning, to the amazement of all beholders.

In less than a quarter of an hour he was back with the palm branch, which, on dismounting, he laid at the feet of the King, whose desire to possess this magic steed was now increased a hundred times, and who offered to pay whatever sum the other demanded.

" Sire," replied the Hindu, " there is only one thing I will take in exchange for this horse, which, as your Majesty perceives, is one of the wonders of the world."

" What is that ? " inquired the King. " Name it, and it is yours."

" The hand of the Princess, your daughter," was the reply, which excited the ridicule of all

who heard—for the Hindu was not only unpleasant in appearance, but at least twice the
age of the King; while the Princess, who was
only fifteen, was as beautiful as she was charming.

Prince Feroze-shah, who stood beside the
King, his father, was extremely indignant.

" I hope, my father," he said, " that you will
not hesitate to refuse such an insolent demand;
and will also chastise the maker of it."

" My son," replied the King, who had a crav-
ing for anything that was rare and curious, " I
have no intention of granting the request. But,
possibly, he is not serious in making it, and
would accept the weight of the horse in gold.
In any case, suppose you mount the horse yourself, and give me your opinion of it."

The Prince was but too willing to agree ; and
the Hindu ran to assist him. But the Prince
mounted without his assistance ; and as soon
as he had his feet in the stirrups, without waiting for any instructions, he turned the peg as
he had seen the other do. Instantly, the horse
rose in the air, as swift as an arrow ; and in a
few moments both horse and rider were out of
sight.

The Hindu, alarmed at what had happened,
prostrated himself before the King, who was

at once angry and alarmed at the disappearance of his son.

" Your Majesty must admit that I was blameless," he said. " The Prince gave me no time to utter a word, or to point out to him a second peg by which the horse is controlled and made to descend. It can also be guided by means of the bridle. But it is possible that the Prince may discover this for himself."

" Your own life shall answer for that of my son," said the King. "And until he returns, or I hear some tidings of him, you shall be put in prison, and fed on bread and water."

Meanwhile, the Prince was being carried so rapidly through the air that in less than an hour he was out of sight of the earth. He then thought it was time to return ; so he pulled the bridle, and turned the peg with which he had started the horse the opposite way. When he found that this had no effect, but that the horse continued to ascend, he became alarmed. He continued to turn the peg one way and another, but without arresting the horse's ascent ; and it seemed as though, in time, he must be burnt up by the sun. Then, to his great joy and relief, he discovered another smaller peg behind the horse's other ear, and, turning this, his upward flight was instantly checked and he began to descend, but at a much slower rate.

The sun was already setting, and it grew dark rapidly as he drew near the earth, so that he was unable to discover what was beneath him—whether a city, a desert, a plain, or a mountain top. It was equally possible that the horse might plunge with him into a lake, or river, or even into the sea. Consequently, when at the dead of night, the horse at last came to a stop, and the Prince felt solid ground beneath his feet, he was inexpressibly relieved. He was also agreeably surprised to find himself on the terrace of a magnificent palace, gleaming with white marble.

He was faint and hungry, having eaten nothing since the early morning, and at first could scarcely stand. But, leaving the horse, he groped his way along until he came to a staircase, which he found led downward, and at the foot of which was a half-open door, through which a ray of light shone.

Descending as noiselessly as possible, the Prince paused at the door and, listening, heard the loud breathing of sleepers within. He advanced cautiously, and by the light of a lamp saw that the sleepers were black slaves. Their naked sabres lay beside them; which was enough to show him that this was the guard chamber of some royal personage.

Proceeding on tiptoe, the Prince crossed the chamber, without waking any of the sleepers, to a curtained archway. Raising the curtain, he saw a magnificent chamber with a raised couch in the centre; while round the sides of the chamber were ranged low couches on which a number of female slaves were sleeping. The Prince crept softly towards the centre couch, and saw the most beautiful Princess in the world sleeping on her silken pillows, with her hair spread round her like a veil.

Falling on his knees, he remained entranced by her loveliness, until the power of his gaze penetrated her closed eyelids, and, opening her eyes, she saw the handsomest Prince in the world regarding her in an ecstasy of admiration.

She showed the greatest surprise, but not the least sign of fear ; observing which, the Prince ventured to address her in the most respectful manner.

" Beautiful Princess," he said, " you see at your feet the Prince of Persia, brought here by what he now regards as a most happy and fortunate adventure, and who implores your aid and protection."

" Prince," she replied, " the kingdom of Bengal,

in which you now are, will afford you all the hospitality and assistance you may require. My father, the Rajah, built this palace not far from his capital for the sake of the country air. Of this place I am absolute mistress, and I bid you welcome. At the same time, though I much desire to know by what means you have arrived here from such a far country as Persia, and by what magic you have evaded the vigilance of my guards, I am convinced that you must be in need of rest and refreshment. I will, therefore, direct my attendants to show you to an apartment where you may obtain both before answering any of the questions which I am dying to put."

Her attendants, though naturally much surprised at the sight of the Prince in their midst, at once carried out her commands; and he was conducted to a handsome room, where, after he had been supplied with the refreshment of which he was so much in need, he slept soundly until morning.

The Princess took great pains with her toilet next day, and altered her mind so often as to what she would wear, and, generally, gave so much trouble to her women that they plainly perceived what a favourable impression the stranger must have produced.

When her mirror assured her that never had

she appeared so charming, she sent for the Prince, and expressed a desire to hear what strange adventure had caused his sudden appearance of the night before.

The Prince was only too pleased to relate the story of the Enchanted Horse and all that had befallen him since he had mounted it. He concluded by thanking her for the kind and hospitable manner in which she had received him, and declaring that it would now be his reluctant duty to return without delay, and relieve the anxiety of his father.

The Princess would not agree to this; but urged him to stay a short time longer, as her guest, in order to see a little of the kingdom of Bengal, where he had so unexpectedly arrived, and of which he would then be better able to give an account on his return to Persia.

The Prince could hardly refuse such a request from such a charming Princess, and so put off his return from day to day, and from week to week; while the Princess entertained him with feasts, concerts, hunting parties, and every other form of amusement she could think of. In this way, the time flew so fast that the Prince was surprised and ashamed when one day he found that two months had passed; during which time his father must either have suffered the greatest possible anxiety, or else have concluded that his son was dead. Not another day would he consent to remain at the Palace; and yet, he asked, how could he tear himself away from his " adorable Princess " ?

The Princess made no reply to this, beyond casting down her eyes and blushing; in spite of which, he went on to ask whether he might dare to hope that she would return to Persia with him ?

Without uttering a word, she gave the Prince to understand that she had not the least objection to this arrangement; though she afterwards admitted a little nervousness in case the Enchanted Horse might refuse to carry a double burden. But the Prince easily reassured her; he also declared that, with the experience he had gained on his journey, he was now quite capable of managing and guiding the Horse as he desired.

The Princess thereupon consented to fly with him; and she arranged matters so that no one should have the slightest suspicion of their intentions.

Consequently, very early the next day, when all the other inhabitants of the palace were still sleeping, she stole from her room to the terrace, where both the Horse and the Prince awaited her.

The Prince turned the Horse towards Persia and, having first mounted himself, assisted the Princess to mount behind him. Then, when she was safely settled, with both her arms round his waist, he turned the peg, and the Horse mounted into the air.

It flew as rapidly with two riders as with one; and in little more than two hours Prince Ferozeshah could distinguish the domes and minarets of the city of Shiraz, from which he had flown on the first day of the New Year.

He thought it better not to fly directly to the palace ; and so alighted at a sort of pavilion, or summer palace, just outside the walls. Here he left the Princess while he went to break the happy news of his return to his father. Leaving the enchanted steed behind, he obtained another horse, on which he rode ; and, being recognized as he passed through the streets, was welcomed with shouts of joy by the people.

The news of his return preceded him, and he was received by the King, his father, with tears of joy. In as few words as possible, the Prince gave an account of all that had befallen him, including his sensations during the flight, his arrival at the palace of the Princess, and all the kindness and hospitality which had been shown to him since.

" If," replied the King, " there were any way by which I could show my gratitude to this lady, I would do it even if it cost me the half of my kingdom."

" My father," replied Prince Feroze-shah, " you have only to consent to my marriage with this charming Princess, in order to assure the happiness of both. Indeed, I felt so sure of your consent that I induced her to accompany me on my return flight; and she is even now waiting for me at the summer palace. Suffer me now to return and assure her that you will gladly welcome her as a daughter."

" Son," replied the King, " I not only consent most heartily, but will myself accompany you thither, and escort her with due honour to my palace, where the marriage shall be celebrated this very day."

He then ordered that the Hindu should be brought from the prison, where he had been closely confined for the last two months, and set before him.

When this had been done, he said: " I swore that your life should answer for that of my son. Thanks be to God, he has now returned in safety. Go, take your Enchanted Horse, and never let me see your face again."

The Hindu had already learned, from those

who had been sent to release him, of the return of the Prince from a far country, accompanied by a Princess, reported to be of great beauty. He was also able to make himself acquainted with the situation of the summer palace, where she was now awaiting the Prince. The King had ordered him to take his Horse and depart; and he now saw a means by which to obey the King, and, at the same time, revenge himself upon the monarch, as well as upon the Prince, to whom he also owed a grudge.

Consequently, while a procession, with instruments of music to accompany it, was being arranged, and a magnificent litter prepared for the Princess, and while the King was putting on his grandest robes, and a feast being hastily set out, the Hindu, without losing an instant, started off for the summer palace, reaching it before the procession had begun to move on its slow and ceremonious way.

He soon discovered the whereabouts of the Princess, and, appearing before her, announced that he came from the Prince of Persia, in order to bring her on the Enchanted Horse into the presence of the King, who with the whole of his court and all the inhabitants of the city, had assembled in the great square of the palace to view the marvel of her flight through the air.

The Princess did not hesitate a moment, but mounted at once; and the Hindu, placing himself before her, with many protestations of respect, turned the peg, and the Horse soared upwards.

At this moment, the King, the Prince and the entire court were about half-way to the summer palace, when, hearing a mocking laugh which seemed to come from overhead, the Prince glanced up. To his great surprise and distress, he saw the Enchanted Horse bearing the Princess and the Hindu high above the heads of the procession, which, on hearing the Prince's cry of anguish, came to a dead stop.

The King also saw and recognized the Hindu, and, furious at this insult to his dignity, hurled imprecations upon him as horse and riders rapidly dwindled to a speck in the sky.

The courtiers and other members of the procession added their voices, and produced such a clamour that it was heard all over the city; but the grief of Prince Feroze-shah was beyond words.

He returned to the Palace, where for a time he shut himself up and refused to see anyone, or to take any food. Then, realizing the uselessness of this behaviour, he obtained the habit of a dervish through a trustworthy agent; for he had formed a plan to disguise himself, and set

out and search for his beloved Princess until
he had found her, or had perished in the attempt.
He knew not which way to go, but trusted Providence to direct him ; so, furnishing himself
with sufficient money and jewels to last a considerable period, he left his father's palace without informing anyone of his purpose.

Meanwhile, the Princess, as soon as she found
that, instead of being conducted to her Prince,
she was being torn from him, had wept and
implored her captor to restore her to her dear
Feroze-shah. It was impossible to escape except
by throwing herself from the horse's back, which
she was loth to do. Thus, after a flight which
lasted through the night, she found herself
early next morning in the kingdom of Cashmere.
The Hindu had descended in a wood outside the
walls of the capital city ; and the Princess now
had a chance of getting help. So, in spite of all
efforts to prevent her, she cried as loudly as she
could, in the hope that someone would hear her
and come to her assistance.

It happened, very fortunately, that the Sultan
of that country, in returning from a hunting
expedition, passed within hearing of her cries,
and went to her rescue.

He saw the Hindu struggling with the Princess, whom, in trying to stifle her voice, he had

half suffocated, and demanded who he was, and why he was ill-treating the lady.

The Hindu, ignorant of the rank of the inquirer, replied insolently: " She is my wife, and I shall treat her as I please ; it is no one's business to interfere."

But the Princess cried: " Do not believe him. I am a Princess of Bengal, and was about to be married to the Prince of Persia when this wicked person, whom I believe to be a magician, carried me off by fraud by means of the Horse you see yonder, which is enchanted. Whoever you are, have compassion on me and save me from this wicked man."

She had no need to urge the Sultan further. Her beauty, dignity and evident distress were all in her favour. Convinced of the truth of her appeal, and enraged by the insolence of the Hindu, the Sultan made a sign to his guards, who at once surrounded the now terrified Hindu, and put an end to his prayers for mercy by cutting off his head.

The Sultan then conducted the Princess to his Palace, where she was sumptuously lodged, and received all the honour due to her beauty and high rank.

The Princess was overjoyed at her escape, and hoped the Sultan would at once take steps to restore her to the Prince of Persia.

But she was bitterly disappointed; for the Sultan, charmed by her appearance and manner, had resolved to marry her himself.

At break of day, she was awakened by the beating of drums, the blowing of trumpets, and other sounds of general rejoicing which had been commanded in honour of the occasion.

Later, when the Sultan came to inquire after the health of the Princess, she asked the meaning of all these festive sounds. When informed that they were part of the festivities in honour of her own marriage, she was struck speechless with dismay; and when the Sultan went on to ask her assent to what had already been arranged, she fainted away—which result the Sultan took to be the effect of extreme joy.

When she came to herself, in order to gain time, she resolved to feign madness. This she did by tearing her clothes and her hair, biting her cushions, and rolling on the floor. She even pretended to attack the Sultan with her finger nails, and alarmed him so much that he quitted her presence hurriedly, and went to give orders to stop the drums beating, and the blowing of the trumpets, and to postpone all further preparations for the marriage.

Several times during the day he sent to inquire

if the strange and violent attack which had so suddenly seized the Princess had passed off, or lessened. But each time he was told there was no improvement, and that whatever change there might be was for the worse.

The next day, as the Princess still talked and acted very violently, the Sultan sent his own physicians, as well as those most famous in the city, to visit the patient and report upon the case. But she not only refused to allow them to feel her pulse, or examine her tongue, but would not even let them approach her ; so they came away looking very wise, but shaking their heads, and declaring that the case was hopeless, and that if they could not cure her, nobody could. In spite of this, the Sultan sent far and wide for other physicians, who came, looked at the Princess (who became more violent at each visit), shook their heads, prescribed for her, and went away looking wiser than ever.

He even sent messengers to other kingdoms, offering munificent rewards and great honour to anyone who could cure the Princess of her malady. But the result was always the same, and the Sultan began to despair ; for all this only made him more and more anxious to marry the Princess.

Meanwhile, Prince Feroze-shah, disguised as

P

a dervish, and plunged in grief, was wandering
about the country, looking for his lost Princess.
He travelled from province to province and from
town to town, inquiring everywhere if anyone
had seen or heard anything of an Enchanted
Horse which could fly through the air, and
describing its two riders. The result was that
most of those he met and spoke with thought
he was out of his mind, and, because he was
handsome and amiable, pitied him.

At last, as he was making his usual inquiries
in a city of Hindustan, he heard the people talking of a certain Princess of Bengal, who was to
have been married to the Sultan of Cashmere
had she not become violently mad on the
marriage day.

At this—for to him it seemed that there could
be only one Princess of Bengal—the Prince at
once set out for the kingdom of Cashmere.

Arriving at the capital, after many days, he
took a humble lodging at an inn, where the
talk again was all of the mysterious mad
Princess with whom the Sultan was so much
in love.

Mention was also made of the Hindu and his
well-merited fate; while the Enchanted Horse,
it was reported, had been placed among the
royal treasures. All these circumstances con-

vinced the Prince of Persia that his lost Princess was found at last; the only difficulty being to reach her presence. And even this was not a difficulty long.

The crowd of physicians who had visited and prescribed in vain for their fair patient, great as it had been, was exaggerated by the gossips of the city; so it appeared to the Prince the easiest thing in the world to add himself to the number.

His beard had grown to quite a respectable length during his travels, and gave him a look of age and wisdom. Thus, he had only to exchange the habit of a dervish for that of a physician to be received at the Palace of the Sultan with civility and respect.

"I have come to cure the Princess," he declared. "Many have tried and failed. If I do not succeed, you may cut off my head."

Some time had elapsed since any fresh physician had appeared at the Palace, and the Sultan had begun to give up hope of the Princess's recovery. He therefore at once gave orders that this new physician, who showed so much faith in his healing powers, should be admitted to his presence. He then informed him that, as the Princess of Bengal could not endure the sight of a physician, he would have to be content with a view of his patient through a lattice in an adjoining chamber to that which she occupied.

In this way, Prince Feroze-shah again caught sight of his beloved Princess after their long separation. She was sitting in a despondent attitude, and singing, with tears in her eyes, a mournful melody in which she lamented her sad fate in being separated from all she loved. It brought tears to his own eyes, and he determined to restore her to health and happiness at any cost.

With this intention, he told the Sultan that he now quite understood the nature of the complaint from which the Princess was suffering, and that he would undertake to cure her. But, he added, it was absolutely necessary to speak with her in private; and, if allowed to do so, he was convinced that he could overcome the violent dislike which she showed to any physician who approached her.

The Sultan was much cheered by this, and ordered that the new physician should be ushered into the presence of the Princess without delay.

Directly the Princess caught sight of what she took to be yet another tiresome physician come to prescribe for her affected madness, she began to go through her usual performance of threatening to attack with teeth and finger nails anyone who attempted to come near enough to feel her pulse, or examine her eyes and complexion.

But the Prince, disregarding this, went straight to her, and, bending in salutation, said, in a low tone, for fear of listeners :

" Oh, my Princess, let your beautiful eyes pierce my disguise and see, in the pretended physician, the Prince of Persia, your faithful Feroze-shah, who has sought you in sorrow which is now turned into joy."

At the sound of the well-known voice, the Princess almost fainted with rapture and relief. But, as the Prince warned her that it was possible that they might be under observation, she made an effort to appear calm. At the same time the Prince of Persia, while briefly acquainting her with his own doings and adventures, and listening to the Princess's story, took care to feel her pulse, and behave in every way like the physician he was impersonating.

He asked her if she knew what had become of the Enchanted Horse, by which he hoped they might both make their escape ; but she could not tell him anything about it. Then, when a plan had been arranged between them, the Prince, thinking it unwise to pay too long a visit, left his supposed patient and went to make his report to the Sultan.

The latter was delighted to hear that a change for the better had already taken place, and promised the supposed physician a great reward if he succeeded in entirely restoring the Princess to health. On the next day the Sultan paid her a visit ; and when the lady, instead of biting the cushions and threatening to tear his beard out by the roots, received him in a most gracious and charming manner, he came away with the conviction that the Prince was the greatest physician in the world. He even wished to have the preparations for the marriage resumed where they had been broken off; but the Prince declared that the Princess was not yet so perfectly restored as he would wish. He asked from what country she had come, and by what means she had travelled to Cashmere ; and the Sultan at once obliged him with the entire story of the Hindu and the Enchanted Horse, as far as he knew it.

The Horse, though he was unacquainted with the use and management of it, the Sultan had ordered to be kept in his treasury, as an object of curiosity and value.

At this, the pretended physician stroked his beard, and assumed an expression of profound wisdom.

" Sire," he said, " I am inclined to think that the principal cause of the trouble is this very

Horse itself. The Princess, having ridden upon the Horse, which, as your Majesty knows, is enchanted, has herself been affected by the enchantment. In order, then, that the improvement which I have been so fortunate as to effect in her condition may continue and be made lasting, it is necessary that I should use a certain incense, the burning of which will disenchant the Horse, and so perfect the cure of the Princess. If your Majesty wishes to see a wonderful sight, and give a great surprise and marvellous entertainment to the people of the city, you will cause the Enchanted Horse to be brought to-morrow to the great square before the Palace, and leave the rest to me."

The Sultan signified his willingness to carry out the directions of this newest and greatest of physicians to the letter, and asked if the Princess should be present on the occasion.

" Most certainly," was the reply. " Let the lady be arrayed as a bride, and adorned with jewels so as to set off her beauty to the greatest advantage."

Thus, early next day, the Enchanted Horse was, by order of the Sultan, brought with great ceremony and beating of drums to the square in front of the Palace.

The news that something rare in the way

of sight-seeing was to be provided had spread through the city, and so great a crowd assembled in the square, that the Sultan's guards had all they could do to keep a space clear round the Horse.

A gallery had been erected on purpose to accommodate the Sultan and his court; and, at the proper moment, the Princess of Bengal, accompanied by a band of ladies of high rank who had been chosen for this service, approached the Horse, and was assisted to mount. The supposed physician then had a number of braziers of lighted charcoal placed at regular intervals round the Horse, into which he now solemnly cast handfuls of incense. With downcast eyes, hands crossed on his breast, and muttering strange words which much impressed the hearers, he paced three times round the Horse, within the circle made by the braziers, which now began to give off thick clouds of perfumed smoke.

In a few seconds these clouds became so thick that neither Horse nor rider was visible. At this moment, for which he had been waiting, the Prince jumped nimbly up behind the Princess and, stretching out his hand, turned the right-hand peg.

Instantly, the Horse rose into the air, and, as the spectators gaped after it, the following words floated down and reached the ear of the Sultan, who was just beginning to surmise that something was wrong.

" The next time the Sultan of Cashmere thinks of marrying a Princess who has come to him for protection, let him make sure that he has the lady's consent."

In this way was the Princess of Bengal rescued from the Palace of the Sultan of Cashmere, and brought the same day to Shiraz, the capital of Persia, where the return of the missing Prince with the lost Princess was greeted with general joy by high and low.

The King of Persia at once sent an ambassador to the father of the Princess, who had for months been mourning the mysterious disappearance of his daughter, to demand his consent to her marriage with Prince Feroze-shah. On that being given, the marriage was celebrated with much magnificence, and the Prince and Princess of Persia lived in honour and happiness for many years.

ALI BABA AND THE FORTY THIEVES

IN a certain town of Persia there lived two brothers, one named Cassim, the other Ali Baba. Cassim had married a wife who brought him a good deal of property, and he had thus become one of the richest merchants in the town.

Ali Baba, on the other hand, who had married for love, and not for money, had to eke out his slender means by cutting wood in a neighbouring forest, and carrying it about the town to sell, on three asses, which were his only possession.

One day, Ali Baba went to the forest, and had very nearly finished cutting as much wood as his asses could carry, when he perceived a thick cloud of dust advancing towards him.

Ali Baba was a cautious man ; so he climbed a tree which grew at the foot of a large rock, and hid himself among the branches, where he could see without being seen.

Presently a band of horsemen appeared. Ali Baba counted forty, all well armed and mounted. Each of them tethered his horse and took off the saddle bags, which seemed extremely heavy.

Then one, whom Ali Baba took to be the captain, came to the rock and exclaimed, "OPEN, SESAME!"[1]

Immediately a door opened in the rock, and they all passed through—the captain going last —and the door closed behind them.

The robbers continued within the rock for some time; and Ali Baba was compelled to remain in the tree, and to wait with patience for their departure, as he was afraid to leave his place of refuge, lest some of them should come out and discover him.

At length the door opened, and the forty robbers came out. The captain, contrary to his former proceeding, made his appearance first. After he had seen all his troop pass out before him, Ali Baba heard him exclaim, "SHUT, SESAME!" and the door closed with a clang. Each man then returned to his horse, put on its bridle, fastened his bag, and mounted. When the captain saw that they were ready, he put himself at their head, and they departed on the road by which they had come.

Ali Baba watched till he could see them no longer, and, in order to be more secure, delayed his descent for a considerable time. As he recollected the words the captain of the robbers had used to open and shut the door, he had

[1] *Sesame* means a small grain.

the curiosity to try if the same effect would be produced by his pronouncing them. He therefore made his way through the bushes to the door they concealed, and, on exclaiming, "OPEN, SESAME!" the door instantly flew wide open.

Ali Baba, who had expected to find only a dark and gloomy cave, was astonished at seeing a large, spacious, well-lighted and vaulted room, dug out of the rock, and so high that he could not touch the roof with his hand. It received light from an opening at the top of the rock. He observed in it a large quantity of provisions, numerous bales of rich merchandise, a store of silk stuffs and brocades, and, besides all this, great quantities of money, both silver and gold, partly piled up in heaps and partly stored in large leather bags, placed one on another.

Ali Baba did not hesitate a moment, but entered the cave. As soon as he was in, the door closed behind him. But, as he knew the magic words by which to open it, this did not worry him. He paid no attention to the silver, but made directly for the gold coin, and particularly that portion which was in the bags. Having collected as much as he thought he could carry, he went in search of his asses, which he had left to look after themselves when he climbed the tree. They had strayed some way, but he brought them close to the door of the rock, and loaded them with the sacks of gold, which he then completely covered with faggots. When he had finished his task he pronounced the words : " SHUT, SESAME ! " The door instantly closed ; for, although it shut of itself every time he went in, it remained open on his coming out till he commanded it to close.

Ali Baba now took the road to the town ; and when he got to his own house drove his asses into the small courtyard belonging to it, and shut the gate with great care. He then carried the bags into his house and emptied them of their contents before his wife, who was first of all struck speechless, and then accused her husband of having turned robber. But her alarm was turned to joy when Ali Baba related his wonderful adventure.

She tried to count the money, but Ali Baba, who was anxious to dig a hole and bury his treasure before any prying eye could see it, declared it would take too long.

" Very well," she said, " dig your hole, and while you are digging it I will go and borrow a measure from my sister-in-law ; for I am determined to know how much money there is."

So, having promised not to breathe a word about the gold, the wife of Ali Baba set off, and went to her brother-in-law, Cassim, who lived a short distance from her house. Cassim was from home ; so she addressed herself to his wife, whom she begged to lend her a small measure for a few minutes.

" With pleasure," said the sister-in-law ; " wait a moment, and I will bring it to you." She went to bring it ; but, knowing the poverty of Ali Baba, she was curious to know what sort of grain his wife wanted to measure ; she bethought herself, therefore, of putting some tallow under the measure, in such a way that it could not be observed.

The wife of Ali Baba returned home, and, placing the measure on the heap of gold, filled and emptied it till she had measured the whole. Her husband having by this time dug the pit for its reception, she informed him how many measures there were, and both rejoiced at the greatness of the treasure. While Ali Baba was burying the gold, his wife carried back the measure to her sister-in-law, without observing that a piece of gold had stuck to the bottom. " Here, sister," said she, " you see I have not kept your measure long ; I am much obliged to you for lending it to me."

So soon as the wife of Ali Baba had gone, Cassim's wife examined the bottom of the measure, and was astonished to see a piece of gold sticking to it.

"What!" she exclaimed, "has Ali Baba such an abundance of gold that he measures, instead of counting it? If so, how in the world did he come by it?"

Her husband, Cassim, was from home, but the moment he entered the house his wife flew to him and said:

"Cassim, you think you are rich, but Ali Baba has infinitely more wealth: he does not count his money as you do, he measures it." Cassim demanded an explanation, and his wife showed him the piece of money she had found sticking to the bottom of the measure.

Far from feeling any pleasure at his brother's good fortune, Cassim felt extremely jealous. The next morning, before sunrise, he went to Ali Baba with the intention of solving the mystery.

"O Ali Baba," said he, " you are very reserved in your affairs: you pretend to be poor, and yet you have so much money that you must measure it."

"O my brother," replied Ali Baba, "I do not understand; pray explain yourself."

"Do not pretend ignorance," answered Cassim; and, showing Ali Baba the piece of gold his wife had given him, he continued: "How many pieces have you like this that my wife found sticking to the bottom of the measure which your wife borrowed from her yesterday ? "

When Ali Baba found that, thanks to his wife, his sudden wealth was a secret no longer, he frankly owned by what chance he had found out the retreat of the thieves, and he offered, if Cassim would agree to keep the secret, to share the treasure with him.

" This I certainly expect you will do," replied Cassim in a haughty tone ; and he added : " but I demand to know also the precise spot where this treasure lies concealed, and the signs which may enable me to visit the place myself. If you refuse this information I will go and inform the police, and you will not only be unable to help yourself to any more money, but you will lose what you have already taken; whereas I shall receive my portion for having informed against you."

Actuated more by natural goodness of heart than by fear of his brother's threats, Ali Baba gave the information demanded, and even told Cassim the words he must pronounce both on entering the cave and on quitting it.

Next morning, before break of day, Cassim, full of the hope of possessing himself of the entire treasure, set off with ten mules furnished with large hampers which he proposed to fill.

He took the road Ali Baba had pointed out,
arrived at the rock, and saw the tree, which,
from the description, he knew to be the one
that had concealed his brother. He soon discovered the door, and pronounced the mystic
words : " OPEN, SESAME ! " The door opened,
he entered, and it immediately closed behind
him. On examining the cave, he found even
more wealth than the description of Ali Baba
had led him to expect. Having feasted his eyes,
he started to collect as much treasure as his ten
mules could carry. But when, dragging a number of sacks behind him, he came to the door,
he found, to his great consternation, that he
had forgotten the right words. "OPEN, BARLEY ! "
he said ; but the door did not budge an inch.
He then named the various other kinds of grain,
all but the right one, but the door did not move.

At this, fear took possession of his mind.
The more he endeavoured to recollect the word
sesame, the more he failed. He threw to the
ground the sacks he had collected, and paced
backward and forward in a perfect frenzy of
terror. The riches which surrounded him had
no longer any charms for his imagination.

Towards noon, the robbers returned to their
cave; and when they saw the mules belonging to
Cassim standing about the rock, laden with

hampers, they were greatly surprised. They all, including the captain, alighted and, drawing their sabres, went towards the door, and pronounced the magic words, which caused it to open.

Cassim, who from inside the cave had heard the noise of horses trampling, felt sure the robbers had arrived, and that his death was certain. Resolved, however, to make one effort to escape, he posted himself near the door, ready to run out as soon as it should open. The word *sesame*, which he had in vain endeavoured to recall, was scarcely pronounced when the portal opened, and he rushed out with such violence that he threw the captain to the ground. He could not, however, avoid the other thieves, who cut him to pieces on the spot.

On entering the cave, the robbers at once discovered the sacks of gold which Cassim had left near the entrance, and replaced them; but they did not notice the absence of those taken by Ali Baba. They were, however, much puzzled as to the means by which Cassim had managed to enter the cave; and, in order to scare off anyone else who might dare to enter, they cut the body of the unfortunate Cassim into quarters, and placed them near the door.

Then they mounted their horses, and set off to commit more robberies.

The wife of Cassim, in the meantime, began to feel very uneasy as night approached, and her husband did not return. She went, in the utmost alarm, to Ali Baba, and said: "O brother, I believe you are well aware that my husband went to the forest, and for what purpose. He has not yet come back, and I fear some accident may have befallen him."

Ali Baba had suspected his brother's intention after the conversation he had held with him. However, he replied that she need not feel any uneasiness, as Cassim most probably thought it wiser not to return until dark. Thus he soothed her alarm so that she returned to her house, and waited patiently till midnight; but after that hour her fears returned with two-fold strength. She spent the night in watching and weeping, and at break of day ran to Ali Baba, and entreated him to go and seek for Cassim.

After advising the disconsolate wife to restrain her grief, Ali Baba immediately set off with his three asses to the forest. As he drew near the rock, he was astonished to observe that blood had been shed near the door, and, not having met on his way either his brother or the ten mules, he looked on this as an unfavourable sign. He reached the rock, and on his pronouncing the words the door opened and he entered, to be struck with horror by the discovery of the body of his brother cut into four quarters. Without losing time in bewailing his fate, he picked up the remains, which he placed on one of his asses, and covered with faggots. The other two asses he quickly loaded with sacks of gold, covering them with more faggots. Then, commanding the door to close, he took the road to the city, taking care to wait at the entrance of the forest until dark, that he might return without being observed. When he got home he left the two asses that were laden with gold in the care of his wife, and, after telling her in a few words what had happened to Cassim, he led the third ass away to his sister-in-law.

Ali Baba knocked at the door, which was opened to him by a female slave named Morgiana. This Morgiana was very sharp and clever, and Ali Baba knew her abilities well. He broke the bad news to her, and then bade her summon her mistress, who came to him in great anxiety. Ali Baba first made her promise to listen calmly to the story he had to tell, and then related all that had happened. " Sister," added he, " here is a great and sudden affliction for you, but you must control your grief and do your crying later ; for we must contrive to bury my brother as though he had died a natural death.

c

I have an idea which, I think, with the help of Morgiana, can be carried out."

At this, the widow of Cassim allowed her sobs to subside, for she was not without common-sense, and listened while Ali Baba coached Morgiana in the part she was to play.

Accordingly, Morgiana, who was as sharp as a needle, assumed a woeful expression and went to the shop of the nearest apothecary, where she asked for a particular medicine which was supposed to cure the most serious ailments.

On the following day Morgiana again went to the apothecary, and, with tears in her eyes, inquired for an essence which it was customary only to administer when the patient was reduced to the last extremity, and when no other remedy had been left untried. " Alas ! " cried she, as she received it from the hands of the apothecary, " I fear this remedy will be of no more use than the other, and I shall lose my beloved master ! "

Moreover, as Ali Baba and his wife were seen going to and from the house of Cassim, in the course of the day, with very long faces, no one was surprised when, towards evening, the piercing cries of the widow and Morgiana announced the death of Cassim.

At a very early hour the next morning, Morgiana, knowing that an old cobbler lived some distance off who was one of the first to open his shop, went out to visit him. Coming up to him, she wished him good day, and put a piece of gold in his hand.

Baba Mustapha, a man well known throughout the city, was naturally of a gay turn of mind, and had always something laughable to say. He examined the piece of money, and seeing that it was gold, said: " This is good wage ; what is to be done ? I am ready to do your bidding."

" Baba Mustapha," said Morgiana to him, " take all your materials for sewing, and come with me ; but I insist on this condition, that you let me put a bandage over your eyes when we have got to a certain place."

At these words Baba Mustapha began to make objections. " Oh, ho ! " said he, " you want me to do something against my conscience or my honour."

But Morgiana interrupted him by putting another piece of gold in his hand. " Allah forbid," she said, " that I should require you to do anything that would hurt your conscience or stain your honour ; only come with me and fear nothing."

Baba Mustapha suffered himself to be led by Morgiana, who bound a handkerchief over his eyes, and brought him to Cassim's house ; nor did she remove the bandage until he was in the chamber where the remains were placed. Then, taking off the covering, she said : " Baba Mustapha, I have brought you hither that you may sew these four quarters together. Lose no time ; and when you have done I will give you another piece of gold."

When Baba Mustapha had finished his gruesome task, Morgiana bound his eyes again, and after giving him the third piece of money, according to promise, and earnestly exhorting him to keep her secret, she conducted him to the place where she had first put on the handkerchief. Here she took the bandage from his eyes, and left him to return to his house, watching him, however, until he was out of sight, lest he should have the curiosity to return and notice her movements.

Then the body of the unfortunate Cassim was washed, perfumed, wrapped in an elegant shroud, and buried with due ceremony.

The widow remained at home to lament and weep with the women of the neighbourhood, who, according to custom, had repaired to her house during the ceremony ; but Morgiana followed the coffin, weeping and tearing her hair.

Ali Baba had a son who had served his apprenticeship with a merchant of good repute. He now placed the young man in charge of the shop which had belonged to Cassim ; while he himself removed with his belongings to his late brother's house, which was larger and more commodious than his own.

Leaving Ali Baba to enjoy his good fortune, we will now return to the forty thieves. On going back to the cave they were amazed and alarmed to find the body of Cassim gone, together with a large portion of their treasure.

" We are discovered," said the captain, " and if we are not very careful, shall lose all the riches we have amassed with so much trouble and fatigue. All we know is that the thief whom we surprised when he was going to make his escape knew the secret of opening the door. But evidently he was not the only one : another must have the same knowledge. And, as we have no reason to suppose that more than two people are acquainted with the secret, having destroyed one, we must not suffer the other to escape. What say you, my brave comrades ? "

The other thirty-nine robbers agreed that it would be advisable to give up every other enterprise, and occupy themselves solely with this affair until they had succeeded.

" Then," resumed the captain, " the first

thing to be done is, that one of you who is bold, courageous, and cunning, should go to the city, unarmed and in the dress of a traveller, and employ all his art to discover if the singular death we inflicted on the culprit we destroyed is being talked about. Then he must find out who this man was, and where he lived. But, in order to prevent his bringing us a false report, which might occasion our total ruin, I propose that the one selected to perform the task shall consent to the penalty of death in case of failure."

Without waiting till his companions should speak, one of the robbers said : " I agree to those terms. If I should fail, you will, at least, remember that I displayed both courage and readiness in my offer to serve the troop."

Amid the commendations of the captain and his companions, the robber disguised himself in such a way that no one could have suspected him of being what he was. He set off at night, and entering the city just as day was dawning, went towards the public bazaar, where he saw only one shop open, and that the shop of Baba Mustapha.

The merry cobbler was seated on his stool ready to begin work. The robber went up to him, and wished him a good morning, saying, " My good man, you rise betimes to your work ;

how is it possible that an old man like you can see clearly at this early hour ? Even if it were broad day, I doubt whether your eyes are good enough to see the stitches you make."

" Whoever you are," replied Baba Mustapha, " you do not know much about me. Old as I am, I have excellent eyes ; and you would have owned as much had you known that not long since I sewed up a dead body as neatly as possible in a place where there was not more light than we have here."

The robber was greatly elated at so soon discovering this important clue. " A dead body ! " replied he with feigned astonishment, to induce the other to proceed. " Why should you want to sew up a dead body ? I suppose you mean that you sewed the shroud in which he was buried." " No, no," said Baba Mustapha, " nothing of the kind. But, anyhow, it is no business of yours."

Upon this, the robber produced a piece of gold, and putting it into Baba Mustapha's hand, said : " Keep your temper and your secret, too, if you like. All the same, if you would care to earn this piece of money, you can do so by showing me the house where you performed this extraordinary piece of needlework."

" Should I feel inclined to grant your request,"

replied Baba Mustapha, holding the piece of money in his hand as if ready to return it, " I assure you I could not do it, for the simple reason that I was blindfolded both coming and going."

" But, at least," resumed the robber, " you must have some idea of the way you went after your eyes were bound. Pray, come with me : I will put a bandage over your eyes at the place where you were blindfolded, and we will walk together along the same streets, and follow the same turnings, which you will probably recollect to have taken ; and, as all labour deserves a reward, here is another piece of gold."

The two pieces of gold were a great temptation to Baba Mustapha.

" Well, well," he said, " I will do my best."

He then conducted the robber to the spot where Morgiana had put the bandage over his eyes. " This is the place," said he, " where my eyes were bound ; and then my face was turned in this direction." The robber, who had his handkerchief ready, tied it over the old man's eyes, and walked by his side, partly leading him, and partly led by him, till Baba Mustapha stopped.

" I think," said he, " I did not go farther than this." He was, in fact, exactly before the house which had once belonged to Cassim, and where

Ali Baba now resided. Before taking the bandage from the cobbler's eyes, the robber quickly made a mark on the door with some chalk he had brought for the purpose ; and, when he had taken the handkerchief off, he asked Baba Mustapha if he knew to whom the house belonged. The cobbler replied that he did not live in that quarter of the town, and therefore could not tell. Whereupon, the robber thanked him, and, when he had seen the cobbler set out for his shop, took the road to the forest, where he felt sure his tidings would be welcome.

Soon after the robber and Baba Mustapha had separated, Morgiana had occasion to go out on some errand ; and when she returned she observed the mark which the robber had made on the door of the house. " What can this mean ? " thought she. " Has anyone a spite against my master, or has it been made only for diversion ? Anyhow, I will take precautions." She therefore procured a piece of chalk ; and as several of the doors on each side of her master's house were of the same appearance, she marked them in the same manner.

In the meantime the thief made the best of his way back to the forest, where he rejoined his companions and related the success of his journey. After some discussion, it was arranged that the spy should return to the city accompanied by the captain and make further investigations.

But, when the two arrived at the house where Ali Baba lived, they were confronted by a whole row of doors with chalk marks, though the robber declared, with an oath, that he had marked but one.

The captain was much annoyed, but there was nothing for it but to return to the forest, where the unlucky robber had his head cut off as the penalty of his failure.

In spite of this, another robber, who flattered himself with hopes of better success, requested to be allowed to see what he could do. Permission being granted, he went to the city, bribed Baba Mustapha with more gold, and the cobbler, with his eyes bound, went through the same performance and led him to the house of Ali Baba.

The thief marked the door with red chalk in a place where it would be less noticed ; thinking this would be a surer method of distinguishing it. But, a short time afterwards, Morgiana went out, as on the preceding day, and on her return the red mark did not escape her sharp eyes. She immediately made a similar mark on all the neighbouring doors.

When he returned to his companions in the

forest, the thief boasted of the precautions he had taken to distinguish the house of Ali Baba, to which he offered to lead the captain without fail. But the result was the same. A whole row of front doors marked with red chalk met the captain's irritated eye; and the second robber lost *his* head.

This reduced the forty thieves to thirty-eight; and the captain determined to undertake the task himself. He therefore went to the city, and, with the assistance of Baba Mustapha, found the house of Ali Baba; but, having no faith in chalk marks, he imprinted the place thoroughly on his memory, looking at it so attentively that he was certain he could not mistake it.

He then returned to the forest, and when he had reached the cave said, " Comrades, I now know with certainty the house of the culprit who is to experience our revenge, and I have planned a first-rate way of dealing with him."

He then charged them to divide into small parties, and go into the neighbouring towns and villages, and there buy nineteen mules and thirty-eight large leathern jars for carrying oil, one of which jars must be full, and all the others empty.

In the course of two or three days the thieves,

having completed their purchases to the captain's satisfaction, he made one of the men, thoroughly armed, enter each jar. He then closed the jars, so that they appeared to be full of oil, leaving, however, a sufficient aperture to admit air for the men to breathe; and, the better to carry out the deception, he rubbed the outside of each jar with oil, which he took from the full one.

Thus prepared, the mules were laden with the thirty-seven robbers, each concealed in a jar, and with the jar that was filled with oil. Then the captain, disguised as an oil merchant, took the road to the city, where the whole procession arrived about an hour after sunset. The captain went straight to the house of Ali Baba, intending to knock and request shelter for the night for himself and his mules. He was, however, spared the trouble of knocking, for he found Ali Baba at the door, enjoying the fresh air after supper. He stopped his mules, and addressing himself to Ali Baba, said: "My good friend, I have brought the oil which you see here from a great distance to sell to-morrow in the market; and at this late hour I do not know where to obtain shelter for the night. If it would not occasion you much inconvenience, do me the favour to take me in, and I shall be greatly obliged."

Although in the forest Ali Baba had seen the man who now spoke to him, and had even heard his voice, he did not recognize him in his disguise.

" You are welcome," he said, and immediately made room for the visitor and his mules to enter. A stable and fodder were made ready for the mules, after which Ali Baba went into the kitchen to desire Morgiana to get supper quickly for a guest who had just arrived, and also to prepare him a chamber and a bed.

The captain of the robbers endeavoured to excuse himself from accepting the bed, alleging that he was loath to be troublesome, but in reality that he might have an opportunity of executing his design with more ease; and it was not until Ali Baba had used the most urgent persuasions that he yielded.

Ali Baba remained with his guest until he saw that he had all he required. Then he wished him good night and said: " You are at liberty to do as you please; you have only to ask for whatever you want; all I have is at your service."

The captain of the robbers thanked him profusely; then, while Ali Baba went into the kitchen to speak to Morgiana, he stole away to the stable, under the pretext of going to see after his mules.

Ali Baba, having again enjoined Morgiana to be attentive to his guest, added : " To-morrow before daybreak I shall go to the bath. Take care that my bathing linen is ready, and give it to Abdalla "—this was the name of his male slave—" and make me some good broth to take when I return."

After giving these orders he went to bed.

The captain of the robbers then found his way to the stable, and gave his men orders what to do. Beginning at the first jar, and going through the whole number, he said to the man in each : " When I throw some stones from the room where I am to be lodged to-night, do not fail to rip open the jar with the knife you are furnished with, and come out : I shall be with you imme- diately afterwards."

He then returned, and was conducted by Mor- giana to the chamber she had prepared for him. Not to create suspicion, he put out the light a short time after, and lay down in his clothes, to be ready to rise as soon as he considered it safe to do so.

Morgiana did not forget Ali Baba's orders. She prepared her master's linen for the bath, and gave it to Abdalla. Then she put the pot on the fire to make the broth ; but while she was skimming it the lamp went out. There was no more oil in the house, and she had not a candle, so she knew not what to do. "What are you worrying about?" said Abdalla. "All you have to do is to go and take some oil out of one of the big jars in the stable."

Morgiana thanked Abdalla for the hint; and, while he retired to bed, she took her own oil jar and went to the stable. As she drew near to the jar that stood first in the row, the thief who was concealed within said in a low voice: "Is it time?"

Any slave but Morgiana would, in the surprise of finding a man in the jar instead of the oil she expected, have jumped and screamed. But Morgiana at once realized the extreme danger in which Ali Baba and his family, as well as herself, were placed. Consequently, she assumed the manner of the captain, and answered: "Not yet, but presently." She then went on to all the vessels in succession, making the same answer to the same question, till she came to the last jar, which was full of oil.

Morgiana by this means discovered that her master had afforded shelter to thirty-eight robbers, including the pretended merchant who was their captain. She quickly filled her own vessel from the last jar, and returned to the kitchen; then, having lighted her lamp, she took a very

D

large kettle, and went again to the stable to fill it with oil from the jar. This kettle she immediately put upon the fire; for she had a plan for the preservation of the family which required the utmost dispatch. As soon as the oil boiled, she took the great kettle and, returning to the stable, poured into each jar, from the first to the last, sufficient boiling oil to stifle and destroy the robber within.

When Morgiana had performed this brave act, she returned to the kitchen, blew out the lamp, and waited to see what would happen.

She had scarcely waited a quarter of an hour, when the captain of the robbers awoke. He got up, opened the window, and gave the signal agreed upon. He listened, but heard nothing. After a while, overcome by uneasiness, he stole from his chamber, and made his way to the stable. On approaching the first jar, he smelt a strong scent of hot oil. He proceeded to the next jar, and to all in succession, and discovered that all his men had shared the same fate; therefore, his plan to revenge himself by the destruction of Ali Baba and all his household had failed, and the sooner he made his own escape the better.

When Morgiana perceived that the captain of the thieves did not return, she rightly concluded that he had decamped through the garden ; consequently, she retired to rest, feeling very well pleased with herself.

When Ali Baba returned from the bath early next morning he was met at the door by Morgiana, who, with an air of mystery, led him to the stable and, pointing to one of the oil jars, begged him to look inside.

He did as she desired ; and, perceiving a man in the jar, uttered a cry of surprise. " Morgiana ! " he exclaimed, " what does this mean ? "

" Look first in all the other jars," she replied.

When Ali Baba had done so, and found a dead robber in each, Morgiana told him the events of the preceding night, how she had discovered and killed the thirty-seven thieves, and of the escape of the captain of the band.

She also informed him of the mysterious chalk marks on the door, and of the manner in which she had made them useless.

When she had finished her tale, Ali Baba, with deep emotion, observed : " You are no longer my slave, but my benefactress. I give you your liberty from this moment, and will soon reward you in a more ample manner. I am convinced that the captain of the robbers laid this snare for me and, through your means, Allah has delivered me. What we have now to do is to use the utmost dispatch in burying the bodies, which we must do with secrecy; and, for this purpose, I will instantly go to work with Abdalla."

Ali Baba's garden was of considerable size, and ended in a clump of large trees. He went, without delay, with his slave, to dig under these trees a ditch, or grave, of sufficient size to contain the bodies. They then took the bodies out of the jars, and placed them in the grave; after which Ali Baba carefully concealed the oil jars. As for the mules, he sent them to the market at different times, and disposed of them by means of his slave.

Meanwhile, the captain of the forty thieves had returned to the forest in a condition of rage and despair, which gradually gave way to a determination to make a final effort to avenge himself upon Ali Baba, whom he held responsible for the destruction of the entire band. Therefore, the very next day, having assumed a fresh disguise, he repaired to the city, where he took a lodging at an inn. As he supposed that the events which had happened in the house of Ali Baba would have become generally known, he asked the host if there were any news stirring; in reply to which the host talked on a variety of subjects, but never mentioned the one the captain had nearest at heart. By this the latter concluded that the reason Ali Baba kept the transaction secret was that he did not wish to divulge the fact of his having access to so immense a treasure.

To carry out his design, the captain provided himself with a horse, which he made use of to convey to his lodging several kinds of rich stuffs and fine linens, bringing them from the cave in the forest at various times. In-order to dispose of this merchandise, he sought for a shop. Having found one that suited him, he hired it, stocked it with his goods, and established himself in it. The shop, as it happened, was exactly opposite the one that had belonged to Cassim, and was now occupied by the son of Ali Baba.

The captain of the robbers, who now assumed the name of Cogia Houssain, took an early opportunity of getting on friendly terms with his neighbours. The son of Ali Baba, being young and of a pleasing address, and the captain having more frequent occasion to converse with him than with the others, the two men soon formed an intimacy. This apparent friendship quickly increased when the captain discovered that the young man was the son of his enemy, Ali Baba.

The son of Ali Baba did not care to receive

favours and hospitality from his new friend without making some return. On mentioning this to his father, Ali Baba willingly undertook to provide an entertainment. " My son," said he, " to-morrow is Friday, when most of the merchants close their shops. I will give orders to Morgiana to prepare a supper to which you shall invite your new friend, Cogia Houssain."

Though the late captain of the forty thieves by this means attained his desire in gaining admission to the house of his enemy, he was most anxious not to take a meal beneath his roof. Therefore, though he entered the house, and received a hearty welcome from Ali Baba, he endeavoured to leave before supper, giving as a reason his dislike to eat of any dish that contained salt. But Ali Baba hospitably refused to accept any excuse. " If that is your only reason," he said, " it need not deprive me of the honour of your company. In the first place, the bread which is eaten in my house does not contain salt ; and as for the meat and other dishes, I promise you there shall be none in those which are placed before you. I will now go to give orders to that effect."

Ali Baba went into the kitchen, and desired Morgiana not to put any salt to the meat she was going to serve for supper. He also told her to prepare, without any salt, two or three other dishes he had ordered.

Morgiana could not refrain from expressing some surprise at this new order. "Who," said she, "is this man who eats no salt with his meat? Your supper will be spoiled if I have to suit his whims."

"Do not be angry," replied Ali Baba; "he is an honest man; do as I desire you."

Morgiana obeyed, though much against her will. She felt a great curiosity to see this man who did not eat salt. So when she had finished her preparations, and Abdalla had prepared the table, she helped to carry in the dishes. On looking at Cogia Houssain, she knew him at once, notwithstanding his disguise, as the captain of the robbers, and she also perceived that he had a dagger concealed under his garment.

"I am not surprised," said she to herself, "that this villain will not eat salt with my master. He is his bitterest enemy, and means to murder him; but I will prevent him."

When Morgiana had finished bringing in the dishes, and assisting Abdalla to wait upon the company, she quitted the room in order to carry out a purpose she had in her mind, leaving Ali Baba, his son, and their guest to enjoy their wine and dessert.

Cogia Houssain, or rather the former captain of the forty thieves, now thought he had a favourable opportunity. " I will make them both drunk," thought he, " and then the son will be unable to prevent my plunging my dagger in the heart of his father ; and I shall escape by way of the garden, as I did before, while the cook and the other slave are at their supper, or, perhaps, asleep in the kitchen."

But, instead of going to supper, Morgiana dressed herself like a dancing girl, and stuck a dagger in her girdle. Then she said to Abdalla, " Take your tambourine, and let us go and entertain our master's guest, and the friend of his son, by the music and dance we sometimes practise together."

Abdalla took his tambourine and accompanied Morgiana to the supper chamber. She then begged her master to allow her to do something to entertain his guest. " A capital idea," observed Ali Baba approvingly.

And though Cogia Houssain would gladly have dispensed with this diversion, he, too, pretended to be highly pleased.

So Abdalla played the tambourine with all the skill he could command, and Morgiana danced. After she had performed several dances with great grace and agility, Morgiana drew out the dagger, and began to flourish it as though this were a part of the performance—sometimes pretending to stab the air, and sometimes herself.

At length, apparently out of breath, she took the tambourine from Abdalla with her left hand, and, holding the dagger in her right, presented the tambourine, with the hollow part upwards, to Ali Baba, in imitation of the professional dancers, who were accustomed in this way to appeal to the liberality of spectators.

Ali Baba threw a piece of gold into the tambourine. Morgiana then presented it to his son, who followed his father's example. Cogia Houssain had already taken a piece of money from his purse, when Morgiana, with a courage and promptness equal to the resolution she had formed, plunged the dagger in his heart.

Ali Baba and his son, terrified at this action, uttered a loud cry.

" Wretch ! " exclaimed Ali Baba, " what hast thou done ? Thou hast ruined me and my family for ever."

" What I have done," replied Morgiana, " is not for your ruin, but for your safety." Then, opening Cogia Houssain's robe to show Ali Baba the dagger which was concealed under it, she continued : " Behold the cruel enemy you had to deal with ! Look at his face attentively,

and you will recognize the pretended oil merchant and the captain of the forty robbers.
Do you not recollect that he refused to eat salt
with you? From the moment you told me
of this, I suspected his design. Are you not convinced that my suspicions were well founded?"

Ali Baba, who now understood the fresh obligation he owed to Morgiana for having thus preserved his life a second time, kissed her on
both cheeks, and said: "Morgiana, I gave you
your freedom, and, at the same time, promised
to show you stronger proofs of my gratitude at
some future period. This period has now arrived.
I present you to my son as his wife."

Then, addressing his son, he continued: "I
believe you to be too dutiful a son to take it
amiss if I bestow Morgiana upon you without
previously consulting your inclinations. Your
obligation to her is not less than mine."

Far from showing any discontent, Ali Baba's
son replied that he willingly consented to the
marriage, not only to prove his ready obedience
to his father's wishes, but because his own in-
clination prompted him to do so.

They then resolved to bury the captain of
the robbers by the side of his former companions; and this duty was performed with
such secrecy that the circumstance was not

known till many years had passed, and no one was any longer interested to keep this memorable history concealed.

A few days after the burial, Ali Baba caused the nuptials of his son and Morgiana to be celebrated. He gave a sumptuous feast, to which he invited all his friends and neighbours; and if the guests felt any surprise at the match, they took care not to show it.

Ali Baba, who had not revisited the cave since he had brought away the body of his brother, Cassim, lest he should meet with any of the thieves and be slain by them, still refrained from going thither even after the death of the thirty-seven robbers and their captain; as he was ignorant of the fate of the other two, and supposed them to be still alive.

At the expiration of a year, however, finding that no attempt had been made to disturb his quiet, he had the curiosity to make a journey to the cave. He mounted his horse; and when he approachd the cave, seeing no traces of either men or horses, he thought this a favourable omen. He dismounted, and fastening his horse, went up to the door and repeated the words: "OPEN, SESAME!" The door opened, and he entered. The state in which everything appeared in the cave led him to judge that no one had been in it from the time when the pretended Cogia Houssain had opened his shop in the city ; and therefore he concluded that the whole troop of robbers was totally dispersed or exterminated ; that he himself was now the only person in the world who was acquainted with the secret of entering the cave, and that consequently the immense treasure it contained was entirely at his disposal. He had provided himself with a bag, and he filled it with as much gold as his horse could carry, with which he returned to the city.

So Ali Baba and his son, whom he took to the cave and taught the secret of entering, lived happily ever after; and their descendants, who were also entrusted with the secret, lived in great splendour, enjoying their riches with moderation, and honoured with the greatest offices of the city.

THE TALKATIVE BARBER

IN the city of Cashgar lived a tailor, who was of an extremely jovial and sociable disposition, and at whose shop a number of people were in the habit of meeting daily to exchange news, and relate stories and adventures. Among them was a barber who had recently come to the city, but who had already made a reputation as a great talker—in fact, when he was present, there was little chance for any other tongue to wag.

One day, when the tailor, as usual, was busily plying his needle and listening to the talk going on around him, he observed a young man, handsome and well dressed, who appeared to be a stranger, and who walked with a limp.

The day was hot, and the young man, pausing at the doorway of the shop, seemed glad to avail himself of the slight shelter which it afforded from the sun.

Seeing this, the tailor politely invited him to enter and rest for a while.

The young man thanked him, entered the shop, and was about to accept the seat offered, when he caught sight of the barber—whose tongue, strange to say, was, for the moment, still.

At once, the pleasing expression of the stranger changed to one of horror and detestation; and, pointing to the barber, he said:

" There is the man to whom I owe my lameness, as well as the ruin of my peace and happiness. It was to escape from his detested presence that some time ago I left the city of Baghdad, and, after visiting several other cities, arrived to-day at Cashgar. I hoped never to see him again; yet it appears that he has arrived here before me. I shall, therefore, at once quit this city, and seek some place where the sight of him will not revive unpleasant memories."

He turned to go; but the tailor and all those present, except the barber, who remained silent, with his eyes fixed on the ground, entreated the young man first to relate the reason of his animosity towards this individual.

" Willingly," he replied; then, turning his back to the barber, he told the following story:—

My father was a well-known and highly-respected citizen of Baghdad. I was his only child; and on his death I inherited the whole of his large fortune. But, so far from squandering it, I conducted myself so well as to gain the esteem of all who knew me.

Up to this time I had rather avoided feminine society, and had made up my mind to remain unmarried, as I considered a single life far preferable.

One day, when I was walking in the street, I saw a number of ladies coming towards me; and, in order to avoid them, I turned into a narrow side street, and sat down upon a bench. Opposite me, in a window, stood a number of very fine flowers. As I was admiring them the window opened, and a young lady appeared, whose beauty had a sudden and most extraordinary effect upon me. She had a watering-pot in her hand, and, as she watered the flowers, she glanced across at me and smiled. After she had tended her flowers, she shut the window, and left me in a state of perturbation which I cannot describe.

A noise in the street brought me to my senses. I turned and saw one of the first cadis of the city approaching, mounted on a mule, and accompanied by five or six of his people. He alighted at the door of the house where the young lady had opened the window; and from this I concluded he was her father.

I returned home in such a state of agitation, caused by this attack of love at first sight, that I was unable to eat or sleep. I became worse and worse, until my relations were alarmed, and sent for a certain wise woman, who was frequently consulted in domestic difficulties. She came and looked at me with a great deal of attention, afterwards begging to be left alone with me.

When the room was cleared she seated herself near my pillow. "My son," said she, "you have hitherto persisted in concealing the cause of your illness; nor do I require you to confess it now; I have sufficient experience to discern that you are love-sick. I can probably accomplish your cure, provided you will tell me the name of the lady who has been able to make a conquest of one generally supposed to be a woman-hater."

I therefore described to her the street where I had seen the lady; and related all the circumstances of my adventure. "If you succeed," continued I, "in obtaining me an interview with this enchanting beauty, you may rely on my gratitude and generosity."

"My son," replied the old woman, "I know the lady. You were quite right in supposing her to be the daughter of the principal cadi in this city; and I am not surprised that you should have fallen in love with such a beautiful creature. At the same time, I must tell you that she is very proud and haughty. It is a pity you did not fall in love with some one else. Still, do not be downhearted. I will do my best."

So she left me in a condition between hope and fear, which resulted in another sleepless night.

When she returned the next day it was with a very long face.

"My son," she said, shaking her head, "it was as I feared. I managed to gain admission to the young lady, and told her of the impression she had made upon you. But, as soon as I ventured to mention your desire for an interview, she showed annoyance and indignation.

"'You are a very insolent old woman,' she said, 'and I will have nothing more to do with you if you say another word on the subject.' But, never mind," continued the old woman, "I am not at the end of my resources."

To cut a long story short, I will only say that the wise woman made several fruitless attempts to soften the heart of the haughty fair one; and I was reduced almost to skin and bone when one day the good soul came to give me new life.

" What present will you make me for the good news I bring you ? " she whispered. I raised myself in my bed, and replied with transport : " The gift shall be worthy of the occasion. What have you to tell me ? "

" Yesterday," she resumed, " I went to the lady with whom you are in love, and found her in very good humour. I at first put on a mournful countenance, uttered a number of sighs, and shed some tears. ' My good mother,' said the lady, ' why are you in such affliction ? ' ' Alas ! my dear lady,' replied I, ' I have just come from the young gentleman of whom I spoke to you the other day, and who is dying for love of you. Why are you so cruel to him ? '

" ' I do not know,' said she, ' why you should accuse me of cruelty. How can I be blamed for his present condition ? '

" ' What ! ' replied I, ' did I not tell you that he saw you watering your flowers, and fell in love with the charms which your mirror reflects every day. And, what with thinking of you night and day, and being unable to eat or sleep, he is reduced to skin and bone; indeed, unless some improvement takes place, I do not think he will live much longer.'

" This startled her, and I saw her change colour.

" ' Is what you say true ? ' she asked, ' and does his illness really proceed only from his love for me ? '

" ' Ah, lady,' replied I, ' it is but too true ! ' ' And do you really think,' resumed she, ' that the hope of seeing and speaking to me would help his recovery ? '

" ' Very probably,' said I. ' Then,' she replied, ' I will allow him an interview; but he must not expect to marry me, unless my father gives his consent.'

" ' O lady,' said I, ' you are very good. I will go and tell the young gentleman that he is to have the delight of seeing and conversing with you."

" ' I do not know,' said she, ' that I can fix a more convenient time for our interview than Friday next, during the midday prayer. Let him observe when my father goes to the mosque; and then let him come immediately to this house. We will converse together during the hour of prayer, and he must leave before my father returns.' "

Whilst the good woman was talking, I began to feel better; and by the time she had concluded, I found myself quite recovered. " Take this," said I, giving her my purse full of gold; " to you alone I owe my cure."

On the appointed morning I rose betimes,

and spent some time reviewing my wardrobe and selecting the handsomest garments it contained. Then I decided that I wanted shaving, and ordered one of my slaves to seek a barber who was expert and quick.

The slave brought me this unlucky barber who is here present. After saluting me, he said : " My master, to judge by your looks I should say you are unwell." I replied that I was recovering from a very severe illness. " May Allah preserve you from all kinds of evils," continued he. " And now tell me what is your pleasure ? I have brought my razors and my lancets ; do you wish me to shave or to bleed you ? "

" Did I not tell you," returned I, " that I am recovering from an illness ? I did not send for you to bleed me. Be quick and shave me, for I have an appointment precisely at noon."

The barber was very slow in spreading out his apparatus and preparing his razors. Instead of putting water into his basin, he drew out of his case a very neat astrolabe, which is an instrument for measuring the height of the sun, and, leaving the room, went into the court to take an observation. On returning, he said. " You will, no doubt, be glad to learn, sir, that this is the eighteenth day of the moon of Safar ;

and that the conjunction of Mars and Mercury signifies that you cannot choose a better time to be shaved than the present day and the present hour. But, on the other side, this conjunction carries with it a bad omen. It demonstrates to me that you will this day encounter a danger; not, indeed, a risk of losing your life, but the peril of an inconvenience which will remain with you all your days. You ought to thank me for warning you, and should be careful accordingly."

I was sincerely vexed at having fallen into the hands of this chatterbox of a barber. "I care very little," said I angrily, "for your advice or your predictions. You came here to shave me; therefore either perform your office or begone, that I may send for another barber."

" My master," replied he, in an unconcerned tone which irritated me still farther, "what reason have you to be angry? Do not you know that all barbers are not like me, and that you would not find another like myself, even if you had him made expressly for you? You only asked for a barber; and in my person you see united the best barber of Baghdad, an experienced physician, a profound chemist, a never-failing astrologer, a finished grammarian, a per-

fect orator, a philosopher, a lawyer, a mathe-
matician—who is also thoroughly accomplished in
geometry, arithmetic, astronomy and algebra,
an historian, a poet, and an architect. There
is nothing in nature concealed from me; and I
am prepared to take you under my protection,
and secure you from all misfortunes with which
the planets may threaten you."

Notwithstanding my anger, I could not help
laughing at this speech. "When," I asked,
"do you mean to stop chattering, and begin
to shave me?"

"Indeed," replied the barber, "you do me
an injury by calling me a chatterer: for you
must know that I everywhere enjoy the honourable appellation of 'Silent.' I have six
brothers, whom you might with some reason
term chatterers. Their names are Bacbouc, Bak-
bara, Bakbac, Alcouz, Alnascher and Schacabac.
One is hump-backed, one toothless, one is half
blind, one is quite blind, one is deaf, and the other
has a defect in his speech. And they are all
great talkers; but I, who am the youngest of
the family, am very grave and sparing of my
words."

"Give him three pieces of gold," I cried, losing
all patience, "and send him away, that I may
be rid of him; I will not be shaved to-day."

"My master," cried the barber, at hearing this, "it was not I who came to seek you; it was you who ordered me to come; and, that being the case, I will not quit your house till I have shaved you."

He then began another speech which lasted a full half-hour.

"In the name of Allah," I said to him, as he paused to take breath, "leave off your fine speeches, and despatch me quickly. I have an affair. of the greatest importance which obliges me to go out at noon. Shave me directly, or leave my house."

When he saw that I was really angry with him, he said: "O master, do not be wrathful; I will begin directly." In fact, he washed my head and began to shave me; but he had not touched me four times with his razor, when he stopped to say: "My master, you are hasty; you should abstain from these gusts of passion, which only do you harm."

"Go on shaving me," said I, "and speak no more. You ought to have finished long since."

"Moderate your impatience," replied he; "perhaps, you have not considered well what you are going to do. I wish you would tell me what this affair is about which you are in such haste, and then I would give you my opinion on it. You have plenty of time; for it will not be noon these three hours."

" Finish shaving me at once," I exclaimed.

But, instead of this, he seized his astrolabe a second time, and left me, half shaved, to go and see precisely what o'clock it was.

" My master," said he on his return, " I was certain I was not mistaken ; it wants three hours to noon, or all the rules of astronomy are false."

" Mercy of Allah ! " cried I, " my patience is exhausted. I can hardly refrain from falling upon thee and strangling thee."

" Be calm, my master," said he coolly, " and you shall be shaved in a moment."

Saying this, he put the astrolabe in its case, took his razor and began to shave me ; but whilst he was shaving he could not help talking. " If," said he, " you would inform me what this affair is that will engage you at noon, I would give you some advice, which you might find serviceable."

To satisfy him, I told him that some friends expected me at noon, to give me a feast and rejoice with me on my recovery.

Directly the barber heard me mention a feast, he exclaimed : " That reminds me that yesterday I invited four or five friends to come to my

house to-day. But I had quite forgotten it, and
have not made any preparations for them."

" Only be quick and finish shaving me," I
replied, " and you shall have all the food that
has been prepared for me to-day; and as much
wine as you want."

He was not content to rely on my word. " May
Allah recompense you," cried he. " But pray
show me these provisions, that I may judge if
there will be enough to regale my friends handsomely."

" I have," said I, " sufficient meat for four
courses."

And I gave orders to a slave to produce the
whole supply, together with four large jugs of
wine.

" This is well," replied the barber, " but we
shall want some fruit for dessert."

I desired my slaves to give him what he
wanted. He left off shaving me to examine
each thing separately; and, as this examination
took up nearly half an hour, I stamped and
raved with impatience; but the rascal did
not hurry the more. At length, however, he
again took up the razor, and for a few minutes
went on shaving me; then, stopping suddenly,
he cried: " I should never have supposed that
you had been of so liberal a turn. Certainly, I

did not deserve the favours you heap on me ; and I assure you that I shall retain an eternal sense of my obligation, as I have nothing but what I get from generous people like yourself. In this I resemble Zantout, who rubs people at the bath, and Sali, who sells little burnt peas about the streets, and Salouz, who sells beans, and Akerscha, who sells herbs, and Abou Mekares, who waters the streets to lay the dust, and Cassem, who belongs to the Caliph's guard. And yet they are all cheerful and contented, envying no one, and ready to dance and sing at every opportunity. If you will allow me, I will now show you exactly how Zantout sings and dances."

The barber sang the song and danced the dance of Zantout ; and, notwithstanding all I could say, he would not stop till he had given a similar imitation of each of the men he had mentioned. After that he said : " Sir, I am going to invite all these good people to my house ; and, if you will take my advice, you will be of our party, and leave your friends, who are, perhaps, great talkers, and will only disturb you by their tiresome conversation."

Notwithstanding my anger, I could not avoid laughing.

" I wish," said I, " that I had no other engagement ; then I would gladly accept your proposal. As it is, I must entreat you to excuse me. Finish shaving me, and hasten away; for, perhaps, your friends are already waiting for you."

"Since you will not come with me," replied the barber, "you must allow me to accompany you. I will carry home the provisions you have given me; my friends shall eat of them, if they like, and I will return immediately."

"In the name of Allah!" I exclaimed, "go to your friends, eat and drink, and enjoy yourselves, and leave me at liberty to go to mine. The place where I am going is not one in which you can be received."

"On the contrary, my master," he replied, "you will much oblige your friends by taking with you a man like me, who has the art of entertaining and making people merry. Say what you will, I am resolved to go, in spite of you."

It was now almost the moment to set out. I determined, therefore, to appear as if I agreed to everything; so, when he had at last finished shaving me, I said: "Take some of my people with you to carry these provisions to your home; then return hither. I will not go without you."

He accordingly went out, and I finished dressing as quickly as possible. I only waited till I heard the last summons to prayers, and then set forth on my errand. But this wretched barber, who seemed aware of my intention, took care only to accompany my people to within sight of his own house. So soon as he had seen them go in, he concealed himself at the corner of the street, to observe and follow me. Accordingly, when I got to the door of the cadi, I turned round, and was enraged to catch sight of him at the end of the street.

The cadi's door was half-open; and when I went in I found the old woman waiting to conduct me into the presence of the object of my admiration. But I had hardly commenced a conversation with her, when we heard a great noise in the street. The young lady ran to the window, and, looking through the blinds, perceived that the cadi, her father, was already returning from prayers. I also looked out, and saw the barber seated exactly opposite the house.

I had now two subjects for alarm—the arrival of the cadi and the presence of the barber. The young lady quieted my fears on the one subject, by telling me that her father very rarely came up to her apartment. All the same, she had prepared the means of my escape, in case of necessity; but the presence of that abominable barber caused me great uneasiness.

As soon as the cadi had returned home, he began beating a slave who had disobeyed him. The slave uttered loud cries, which could be plainly heard in the street. The barber thought I was the person who was being ill-treated, and that these were my cries. Fully persuaded of this, he began to call out as loudly as he could. He tore his clothes, threw dust upon his head, and shouted for help to all the neighbours, who came running out of their houses. They inquired what was the matter. "Matter enough," exclaimed the barber; "they are murdering my master."

He then ran to my house, and returned followed by all my servants, armed with sticks. They knocked furiously at the door of the cadi, who sent a slave to know what the noise meant. But the slave returned in a state of alarm to his master.

"My lord," said he, "a number of men are trying to force their way into the house, and are already beginning to break open the door."

The cadi himself ran to the door, and inquired what the people wanted. His venerable appearance did not inspire my people with any respect, and they shouted insolently: "What has our master done to you that you are trying to murder him ? "

" My good friends," replied the cadi, " why should I murder your master, whom I do not even know ? My door is open ; you may come in and search my house."

" You have been beating him," said the barber ; " I heard his cries not a minute ago."

" But how," persisted the cadi, " can your master have offended me, that I should ill-treat him thus ? Is he in my house ? And if he is here, how could he get in, or who could have admitted him ? "

" You will not make me believe you, for all your great beard, you old villain ! " cried the barber. " Your daughter and our master are in love with each other, and arranged to meet during the midday prayers. You must have found this out, and returned quickly ; you surprised him here, and ordered your slaves to give him the bastinado. Set him free directly, or we will come and take him."

" There is no occasion," said the cadi, " to make such a riot. If what you say is true, you have only to go in and search for your master."

Directly the cadi had spoken these words, the barber and my servants burst into the house, and began to ransack every corner in search of me.

As I had heard every word the barber said to the cadi, I tried to find some place in which I might conceal myself. The only hiding-place I could discover was a large, empty chest, into which I crept, and shut the lid down upon myself. After the barber had searched every other place, he at last came into the apartment where I lay. He ran directly to the chest, and opened it ; and finding me crouching there, he took it up and carried it away upon his head. He rushed down the staircase into a court, and so reached the street.

As he was carrying me along, the lid of the chest unfortunately opened. I had not resolution enough to bear the shame and disgrace of my exposure to the crowd who followed us, and jumped out so hastily that I hurt myself seriously, and have been lame ever since.

I did not at first feel the full extent of the injury I had suffered; and was able to get up and run away from the people who were laughing at me. I scattered among them a handful or two of gold and silver, and, while they were stopping to pick it up, made my escape by hurrying through several quiet streets. But the wretched barber followed me closely, and never once lost sight of me ; and, as he followed me, he continued calling aloud : " Stop, my master !

Why do you run so fast ? All that has happened to you is your own fault ; and I know not what would have become of you if I had not determined to follow you. I pray you, wait for me."

This put me into such a rage that I could have stopped and strangled him ; but that would only have increased my difficulties. I therefore went into an inn, the master of which was known to me, and said, " In the name of Allah! prevent that mad fellow from following me in here."

He promised to do so, and he kept his word, though not without great difficulty. As it was, this abominable barber abused me violently for what he termed my ingratitude, and told everyone he met the great service he pretended to have done me.

Thus I got rid of him. I knew that if I returned to my own house, either the barber would pester me to death, or else I should be driven to kill him ; therefore, in spite of the poorness of the accommodation, I remained at the inn until I had to some extent recovered from my injury. But, after what had happened to me, I determined to leave the city where I was known.

So, having arranged my affairs, I set out from Baghdad, and arrived here. I had every reason to hope I should be free from this detestable barber in a country so distant from my own. You may judge of my feelings when I now discover, in your company, the man who is responsible both for my lameness and for the abrupt ending of a love affair which might have terminated in a happy marriage; and who has also made me an object of ridicule to the whole city."

With that the young man rose and went out.

"All the same," remarked the barber, as soon as the other was out of hearing. "I maintain that I was perfectly right in acting as I did. And he who has just left us is the most ungrateful of men."